THE ULTIMATES

Some People Aren't Just Ordinary

HRISHIKA PAL

PARTRIDGE

ISBN: Hardcover   978-1-4828-8765-5
             Softcover   978-1-4828-8764-8
             eBook   978-1-4828-8763-1

To order additional copies of this book, contact
Partridge India
000 800 10062 62
orders.india@partridgepublishing.com

www.partridgepublishing.com/india

CONTENTS

Acknowledgments

First of all to my dad for believing in me
Then to my loving family for supporting me
To Kiran uncle who took time off his busy
schedule to help with the editing process
To my English teacher Adrian sir for encouraging
me as well as giving me his advice and suggestions
To my friends Kripa, Veda, Anusha, Rithika
and Archita for reviewing my book
Last but not the least to my publisher Kathy
Lorenzo for being patient with me throughout.

Without these people, this book wouldn't be in your hand right now and this story would have just remained as another mere idea in the back of my head.

PART 1

Chapter 1

The Mysterious Voice

Your name is Jane
Your helper will be Anne
In your quest you may suffer pain
But you have only one aim
To fight him

Tring tring.... wait what was that? I mean the mysterious voice. It sounded like a male voice and a voice I definitely have not heard before. Although the voice did seem familiar in an odd way. Well, my alarm just rang which means it's seven already.

My name is Jane and that mysterious voice was someone else but who?. Lost in thought I quickly did my morning chores and then looking into the mirror I saw brunette hair, jet black eyes and with a height of 5'8.

I called up Anne, as the voice said that she'll be my helper. Anne and I are best friends from... I don't remember exactly but as far as I remember maybe from the time I was born.

I was imagining Anne here with her golden blonde hair, striking light blue eyes and her natural beige skin tone while I had more tan than she did giving me a warm beige skin tone. Also Anne was an inch shorter than I was making her 5'7.

Although our views weren't alike we are so close to each other. Maybe the fact that opposites attract is true. Even though one of the few similarities both of us had was that we were both well built.

As Anne picked up the phone I told her about the mysterious voice and waited for an answer but she remained silent. Wait, did I mention that Anne is super smart? Finally breaking the silence, I asked if she had found anything however to my surprise she said "No".

After what seemed like a minute or two she said "Jane as of now there are two things to find out who the "him" is and what is the quest about. Then eventually we'll also find out about the mysterious voice".

Anne then came over and we discussed on what are next step should be. We tried using Google and even checked out some books however they were of no use.

Then we decided to go out, hoping to gather some more information. But just as we stepped out all of a sudden everything blacked out…

On getting my senses back I realized that I was inside a room and Anne was right beside me. The room was warm and cozy but the weird part was that there were lots of eyes staring at us.

There were boys and girls most of them being thirteen to seventeen; me being fifteen. There wasn't enough light yet I could tell they were all wearing similar clothes only the t- shirts varying from shades of red, blue and green.

Anyway after a while I stopped looking around and finally decided to blurt my questions at everyone present in the room. "Who are you? Why did you bring us here? Have we done anything wrong?" was how I started off.

I could go on forever until a soft and gentle voice interrupted me and said "Don't worry, just relax every thing's going to be fine". She was around her twenties with coppery red hair and gentle hazel eyes. She had pale skin which made her red hair stand out in the crowd along with a thin frame.

Consequently she introduced herself "I am Ellie and don't you worry you haven't done anything wrong. You have come to our *L'Abri* which means home. So in other words this is our home and from now on it is yours as well. This is a place for people like us, this is a home to all the **"Ultimates"!**. We all train here, learn and live together with our type. You are here because you've got our symbol and are now one of us".

Becoming curious I immediately asked "What symbol are you talking about?"

Ellie then replied "*The symbol of the Ultimates, our lightning bolt.* See Anne you have got one near the side of your eye, intelligent aren't you?". To that Anne just blushed.

I was surprised as I had never noticed a lightning bolt on Anne and neither did I ever see one on myself. But then something striking caught my eyes, and alas it was a lightning bolt in my palm. Ellie noticed that too and said, "You are brave Jane." Though I was still perplexed and on seeing my confused expression Ellie explained that the lightning bolt only appeared when the time was right.

Then Anne asked "Where have you got your lightning bolt Ellie?" "I've got mine on my arm" replied Ellie.

"These are the three sacred places our lightning bolt is placed. Depending on where our lightning bolt is placed we are divided into three houses. If the lightning bolt is placed near our eye we belong to the Intelligent House. If the lightning bolt is placed on our palm, then we belong to the Daring and if placed on our arm we go to the Caring house. Blue goes to the Intelligent while Red goes to the Daring and Green goes to the Caring explained Ellie.

Now let me take you for a tour around l'Abri". So as we followed Ellie she showed us the fighting arena where they had all sorts of weapons. This place already got my nerves buzzing. Then Ellie took us to the library actually an ultra huge library I would say. And I could also tell that Anne adored it. As Ellie continued she showed us a nice little farm and right behind there was a forest, where lots of tree nymphs were chatting.

Ellie then said "The tree nymphs are a friend to our kind. We promise to protect them from the outside world because they believe that if they ever left L'Abri they would soon become extinct. Hence in return they provide and make food for us"

As we kept on moving along with Ellie, she showed us three huge houses. Each of the houses represented their own colour. Right behind there was a huge university where they would all gather up, study together, share daily life experiences, etc. Ellie also told us there was a hospital around that corner and a cafeteria right beside that.

"That's it for today girls you must be really tired, why don't we have a nice talk in my office which is that big house straight ahead. Just go change, freshen up and hot cocoa will be waiting for both of you" saying this Ellie was gone.

I was definitely tired and so was Anne. So we went to our respective houses.

I was welcomed with a huge applause and the house was covered in reds and oranges. Every one looked friendly and Bryan who was the head of the house had a jovial nature too

He was taller and older than me about 6'1 and maybe seventeen or eighteen. He was well built with broad shoulders and his shirt which hugged his muscles. But what caught me off gaurd were his deep blue eyes.

"Checking me out?" he said getting me back to reality. "No" I replied rather hastily and also kind of offended. Checking guys out wasn't my thing but it was true I did observe people and their features. He showed me my bed and clothes, I washed my face, thanked Bryan and then waited for Anne to come out. I somehow started to like this place and felt like as if I belonged here.

Anne on the other hand was also welcomed with an applause. Her house was coloured with blues and violets. Books filled her entire room along with some old manuscripts. She loved her new home and met her head of the house who was Abner.

Anne briefly saw that Abner had curly hair, glasses, was about 5'9 and although he did have broad shoulders he wasn't built with too much muscle. He showed Anne, her bed, her clothes and her books. Anne smiled and thanked Abner. After freshening up, Anne came out of the house and met up with Jane.

I asked Anne "Are you liking this place?".

"Jane, I really love this place and my house is so nice with everyone being friendly. But Jane I'm just a bit nervous about going to Ellie's office do you think she'll ask us too many questions?"

To what Anne just said, I didn't know if this was the right place. I mean nothing has happened yet and everybody did seem nice. But was this the right thing to do?. Would I ever be able to get back to my parents?. What if I messed up and what if all of this was just a huge mistake?.

Anne's voice then brought me back to reality when she said "Jane?". Leaving my thoughts aside and trying to sound braver than I felt, I quickly said "Anne, just relax, Ellie seemed so sweet and after all, she only invited us for a talk with hot cocoa".

Anne just listened and we both headed towards Ellie's office.

CHAPTER 2

SACRE

As we reached the office and opened the door, I realized that it looked so much bigger from inside with Ellie seated at her desk.

"Welcome girls have a seat, I'll just bring the hot cocoa" Ellie said as she made her way inside. While we waited for the cocoa to arrive, I noticed that the entire office comprised of reds, blues and greens each representing three of the houses. On one of the walls there were many photos and portraits of old headmasters of L'Abri along with the heads of each house.

As Ellie came back, she held a tray with 3 cups of hot cocoa and some cookies saying

"Please serve yourself".

To that Anne and I both took a cup of hot cocoa while munching on some cookies. Ellie then said "I would like to know if anything strange has happened during the previous week or day anything at all, anything different."

So I began first saying "So you see Ellie like yesterday night I had a strange voice in my head saying something which I think is rather serious".

> *Your name is Jane*
> *Your helper will be Anne*
> *In your quest you may have pain*
> *But you have only one aim*
> *To fight him*

"Hmm" lost in thought Ellie seemed to be thinking hard.

"Jane, for one thing, is certain that you have huge responsibilities in your hand. But unfortunately, I'm not the right person to decide. However, before we go somewhere else, let's hear from Anne".

Anne was reluctant as well as a bit nervous to express her feelings and started slowly.

"So Ellie I have been having bad dreams from the past few days you see". I don't know who is talking, but I know it's a man in addition to that I can also tell you that his intentions don't seem to be very good either.

"What does he say Anne?" asked Ellie.

To that Anne replied "He keeps saying come *join me, together we can rule with your intelligence and my strength come, come to me*".

"Anne!" I cried out and just as I was about to strangle her I said "Why didn't you tell me this earlier? Come-on Anne I am your friend".

"Jane..." she began "I'm really sorry I think I should have told you this before, but I was nervous and scared all at the same time".

"Ellie, don't you think our visions are kind of related?" Anne stated.

"Maybe the guy who he is talking to me, is the guy we have to fight against".

Honestly, I didn't get a word on what Anne was talking about, but looking at Ellie's face, it seemed that she understood what Anne was saying.

Ellie finally stood and said "I won't say anything now we need to ask Sacre".

"Who is Sacre?" Anne and I chorused together.

"I tell you on the way, first let's go to the attic in the university" Ellie said.

As we headed out from Ellie's office she began to tell us about Sacre.

"Sacre is the creator of our L'Abri. He was the first Ultimate. We call him Sacre because it means sacred and to pay him respect. Although he is very old, he is still alive in form of a spirit. He was a French man thus most of our original names are derived from French. His last wish was to look after l'Abri which he continues to do even today. He guides us when we need his help".

In the meantime we had taken the elevator to the topmost floor of the university after we climbed a few stairs and reached the bottom of the attic. This place already gave me the creeps. It had cobwebs, spiders, lizards, rats etc everywhere. As we entered, Anne screamed loudly as a huge black spider appeared right in front of her face. Insects terrified Anne and she was definitely getting freaked out of this place.

Luckily Ellie was leading our path. We had to get higher where lots of stairs were waiting for us. As we took each step there were creaking noises. Time passed and it felt like forever until we finally reached the top. As we reached the top I saw a huge wooden box with a ruby shining on it, right in the middle of the attic floor with a layer of dust covering it.

Then Ellie said she had to go back as it was part of the rules. As I turned to wave a goodbye to Ellie I saw Anne almost in tears. I assured Anne that everything was going to be okay well at least that's what I hoped.

Suddenly Anne said "Look Jane, did you notice that there is no lock on the box and instead just the ruby?".

I was surprised, but at the same time impressed by Anne's observation. I waited for something to happen and so did Anne. We waited for some more time and then Anne said "Maybe Sacre is hiding somewhere and we have to find him".

"Now Anne, do you think we are gonna play hide and seek here?" I said impatiently.

To Anne replied "No Jane lets call out for Sacre. "Sacre can you please help us in our quest?" Anne asked.

There was utter silence in the room when all of a sudden we saw a lot of mist coming out from the ruby. Now the room was filled with teal coloured mist and then the teal mist started to speak to Anne and me.

It said "Good evening girls I'm Sacre. What do you seek?". Anne and I, were both flabbergasted to hear the teal mist speak. And more over Sacre sounded like the exact same mysterious voice.

Then I asked "Sacre can you please help us in our quest?".

"Oh, Of course, after all I was the one who told you about the quest," was Sacre's reply.

"Really?" asked Anne "Then were you the one who asked me to help you?"

It was now Sacre's turn to be confused,

Sacre then said "Dear Anne, can you please tell me what you are talking about?".

So then Anne told Sacre about the voice which she heard in her dream.

"Come join me, together we can rule the world with your intelligence and my power. Come, come to me". Sacre was silent for a while and then said,

"Anne my dear, this is something very dangerous and may lead you to the Presage".

"Wait Presage? Aren't sages suppose to be a good thing?" I asked perplexed.

"Jane it's actually a French word for a bad omen" was what Sacre said

Anne started saying "Sacre, I was just thinking if the "him" is whom we have to fight against?". Then, instead of saying something very serious which I was expecting, Sacre just laughed and said "Anne you really are very intelligent. And also to what you just said I'm rather afraid that it could be true".

"Sacre what about what you told me?" I asked. "See Jane I can only guide you to some extent, then the choice is yours. The "him" is a very strong evil power that lies in the underworld. He will definitely do something bad to harm all of us and this is inevitable. You'll have to find him and defeat him not by one or two powers but by many. *Soon, let Audacieux, Malin and Soins unite".*

Those were Sacre's last words afterward all the mist disappeared back into the ruby leaving Anne and me alone in the attic, dark and quiet once again.

Both of us went down as quickly as we could, not wanting to stay there even for a second longer. As we reached the bottom we both went to our respective houses. On entering my house I saw everyone fast asleep and without trying to disturb anyone I changed my clothes and I dozed off even before I hit the pillow.

As Anne slept, she started dreaming and they were not ordinary dreams instead they seemed to look like dark nightmares. In her dream the sky turned black haunting her, until she realized the same voice started to speak in her head saying

"Come join me, together we can rule the world, your intelligence and my power. Come, come to me".

Now this time Anne tried to speak back to the voice and said *"No! Whoever you are I am not helping you".*

Now the voice getting angry said *"Oh really you won't come? Fine then I'll force you to come to me Bwahhahhha!!!".*

This frightened Anne but realizing that there was nothing that she could do at the moment she tried to go back to sleep along with which she decided to tell Jane about this in the morning. When Anne got up Abner asked her if she had a good sleep, but Anne lied and happily said that she had a wonderful sleep. Abner then told Anne to go to the cafeteria for breakfast.

Chapter 3

A Terrible Surprise

As all of us in the houses made our way towards the cafeteria, I noticed that each of the houses had their own tables. The food was delicious moreover only then I realized how hungry I was since Anne and I had missed dinner last night. There was toast, butter, jam, corn, bacon, cereals, oatmeal, pancakes, maple syrup, fruits, juices and milk.

Everything seemed to be pretty normal until all of a sudden someone from the Caring house came and screamed "Oh no! Horrible this can't happen".

Then all of us alarmed in unison asked "What happened?".

"Ellie is gone, Ellie isn't there!" soon after which he fainted.

At this chaos broke out everywhere. All the house leaders told everyone to assemble in the auditorium in the university. As we all assembled at the university each of the house leaders Cara from Caring, Bryan from Daring and Abner from Intelligent tried to settle us all down.

There were lots of questions from everyone, but the leaders looked baffled themselves. Then Bryan asked if anyone had any idea of Ellie's disappearance, however all of us only shook our heads looking at one another, until I saw Anne raise her hand, she signaled with her eyes for me to raise my hand up too.

Following Anne's signal I too raised my hand although I had no idea what so ever. Everyone started to give us nasty looks in fact many thought we had held Ellie captive.

Anne announced that finding Ellie, was a quest in itself. To this Bryan said

"Say no more we must talk in private, meet us at the big office".

All other Ultimates were instructed to go to their respective houses until things got settled while Anne and I walked towards the big office.

On reaching the big office I gave Anne a confused look and she said,

"I'll explain everything later".

I didn't want to say anything more, as undoubtedly she looked tense. Cara, Abner and Bryan came in asking the obvious question ; what we had to do with Ellie's disappearance.

Anne then started to cry and said "I'm so sorry it's all my fault".

I was baffled what did Anne have to do with Ellie's disappearance?. Cara, immediately put her hands around Anne starting to comfort her letting Anne know that everything was going to be all okay.

Cara had olive skin with her black hair falling behind her in beautiful waves. So when Anne became comfortable, she told us about the voice that had spoken to her in her dream, in addition to which the voice also told her that she would be to be forced to come to him

Then Abner said "So it's most likely that he took Ellie, but don't worry Anne you did the most logical thing and it isn't your fault".

Even I thought of that and it did make sense. Then I informed the three of them that we had visited Sacre and about the quest.

I also asked them about the powers that Sacre had mentioned about uniting Audacieux, Malin and Soins.

To that Bryan said "They were the ancient names for our houses Audacieux meaning brave Malin meaning intelligent and Soins meaning caring.

Then Anne asked "What are the powers?".

Cara then said "Anne, all of us have power within ourselves, however only some of us recognize them while the others cannot.

"As of now what seems to be the best way out of this is to go to Sacre for help and how to start off" suggested Abner.

Then again we went to the university, then the base of the attic and again climbed up the stairs until we finally reached the top. Cara then said that we had to go alone as this wasn't their quest moreover they couldn't break the rules.

Bryan who seemed to be more laid back said "Chill Cara"

Although on the other hand Abner said "No Cara's right, but this is a different situation and I think we must stay".

As we called out to Sacre tele mist filled the room once again.

Sacre said *"Go to the depths of the underworld where darkness lurks. The spirit lies only there hence you shall find all your answers"* after which Sacre went back inside the ruby.

On our way down Bryan said, "Both of you need some amount of training to go on your quest".

So Bryan and I went to the fighting arena while Cara, Abner and Anne went the other way. Different kinds of weapons were neatly stacked near the arena. Bryan then asked me to pick up any weapon of my choice.

At first I took a knife, but it did not feel right. It felt small in my palm. The bow and arrow caught my eyes, and seemed to be perfect in the first look, although just as I released the arrow Bryan said it will never work as I didn't have any patience to take an accurate aim, so I left that idea.

Then I looked at the gun, yet didn't even try it because I always thought it was such a bother to reload the gun. I picked up the sword, which was light, swift and fast and had the perfect grip, it felt like as if it was made for me.

Now that I had a weapon of my choice, Bryan chipped in and taught me how to use it in a correct manner and also taught me how to apply the right amount of force. In fact we even had a tiring sparring session later. After the practice was over Bryan challenged me to a sword fight. I knew I would lose although it wouldn't hurt to give it a shot. We started and within the next minute I already ended up with a few cuts and bruises but I still continued to fight for longer realizing that I wasn't that bad after all.

After the fight had ended Bryan said "Not bad Jane you did pretty well".

I thanked Bryan for the compliment. Suddenly I felt hungry hoping it was time for lunch. I made my way towards the cafeteria along with Bryan.

In the cafeteria everyone seemed to be calmer than before, although there definitely was an awkward silence. After I finished lunch, I went to Anne where she asked me to get my clothes and food ready for the quest from Cara. She also added that we shouldn't delay and should start as quickly as possible. In fact we should probably start by tomorrow morning itself.

I nodded in reply and asked Anne to go to fighting arena to choose her weapon.

Immediately Anne said, "No, I hate violence, I don't even want a weapon".

I told Anne that it wasn't an option as there was no way she could go in the quest without a weapon. Moreover just to encourage her I told her that I had gotten a sword.

Giving a sigh Anne said "Fine, I'll also give it a try".

I wished Anne best of luck and I headed towards Cara to get my food and clothes ready.

Anne reached the fighting arena, where she saw Bryan waiting.. At first Anne picked up the sword, but it was way too heavy neither did it look good. She then tried the knife, however even that didn't suit her much. Anne continued to try different weapons, until she concluded that nothing suited her.

Bryan who was getting slightly impatient suggested "Why don't you try the bow and arrow?".

So Anne went ahead and tried the bow and arrow, with which she was perfectly at ease! She had all the concentration and patience required for releasing the arrow. Although at the beginning it took her some time to get a hang of it but after a while there was no stopping her. Each time she aimed and shot, she always got the bull's eye!

Even Bryan was impressed with Anne's performance.

Now both Anne and I had got our weapons along with which I also got my red bag ready and placed it next Anne's blue bag. I thought of having a nap as the practice in the fighting arena had really tired me out.

Chapter 4

The Special Gift

Anne was really excited to meet Jane and tell her all about her weapon. As she started looking for Jane, she stumbled into Abner,

who said, "Oh! Hello Anne, could you please do me a favor?".

Anne, who was delighted to have some work said "Yes of course Abner, what is it?".

Then Abner replied "See Anne I have spent a lot of time in the library trying to gather more information about the quest and I would like to share it with all of you, so I am holding a meeting at the big office for the five of us right after dinner. It would be great if you could attend and also inform Cara and Jane about the meeting?".

"Okay, I'll do that, but I haven't seen any of them lately do you know where they are?" Anne asked "I think I saw Cara at the hospital although I am not sure about Jane's whereabouts. Anyways thank you Anne for agreeing to come".

Anne decided to go meet Cara at the hospital. She saw Cara coming out of the hospital and started waving. Cara noticed Anne waving at her consequently waved back. Anne ran towards Cara firstly she told her about the meeting and then asked if she had seen Jane lately. Although Cara thought that having a meeting was a brilliant idea she hadn't seen Jane either.

"What do you want to do Anne?".

Anne being clueless said "I have no idea".

Cara who had something in mind asked "Have you met the tree nymphs in the forest?".

Now Anne remembered something Ellie mentioned about them, that they lived in the forest behind the farm. Having never met them Anne thought it would be a wonderful idea to meet them. As they reached the forest Anne saw some green human like figures moving around. It was very hard to spot them as easily camouflaged among the trees and bushes however on seeing Cara they all came out.

"Anne please meet my friends, the tree nymphs". Cara introduced them to Anne after which she started to talk to them. Soon they were all talking about the flowers and leaves and how beautiful they are in the tree nymphs eye. After sometime Cara said she had to go as she had some work, although Anne decided to stay with the tree nymphs.

The tree nymphs and Anne became friends in no time. Anne then asked "What's the matter why are you all feeling down?". The tree nymphs who felt sad said "We all look sad because we all feel lonely and very disappointed at the way the humans cut the trees and destroy mother nature".

On hearing this Anne felt a pang in her heart and said "Don't worry we all will start to plant trees and if not everyone at least I'll plant trees and plants with my friends and I'll keep visiting you".

Then to cheer them up Anne also told them some jokes, everyone laughed and enjoyed thoroughly. They all had a wonderful time together, but as Anne saw it was getting dark she decided to go. Then the tree nymphs felt bad but happy as well because they had so much fun along with which they have also found a new friend.

They were very delighted and said they'll give Anne a special gift. At first Anne hesitated, however as they gave her the special gift Anne couldn't resist. The tree nymphs gifted Anne a beautiful garland made from lots of colourful flowers.

One the tree nymphs said "Anne my dear, this is no ordinary garland, this garland can answer any of your questions, but beware to use it only for the good and wise. Oh, and one more thing to remember you can only use it once after which all the flowers will fall".

Keeping this in mind Anne was very happy and knew she would use it to find Ellie. As she walked away, she thanked them for their marvelous gift moreover she also promised to visit them once again. She put the garland around her neck and magically it disappeared into her skin.

Anne then thought, how she could possibly use the invisible garland, just as she turned around to ask the tree nymphs.

They said "Anne think of us and your garland will show up and then ask the garland your question".

Anne thanked them once again after which she headed towards the cafeteria. Anne soon reached the cafeteria and saw only a few people moving around. She finally spotted Jane and was overjoyed.

I was shocked to see Anne in such a happy mood who came running towards me.

"Jane, Jane I've got to tell you so much!!!" said Anne.

"Okay, okay Anne you can tell me everything right now I don't really see many of people as we are early" I said.

So then Anne began to tell me everything that happened from the time I wished her luck to choose her a weapon, to the time when we again met in the cafeteria, she told me everything including the upcoming meeting. I was shocked by the fact that so much had happened as I took a nap.

Then curious to see the garland I asked Anne to show it to me. Anne then told me it was having seeped into her skin and would take it out only when the time is right. Just to tease Anne and have some fun, I asked, "Anne are you sure it's within your skin, you might have as well dropped it on your way, because I did see something fall on to the ground when you came running towards me".

Hearing this, at first Anne turned pale, but then realized she saw it seep into her skin and said, "Jane please never ever try to scare me again".

Then, as I saw more Ultimates coming in, I told Anne to hurry up as we didn't want to get late for the meeting. So Anne and I had our dinner as fast as we could and together we went to the big office.

Chapter 5

The Meeting

As we reached the big office, we saw Abner surrounded by lots of manuscripts and books. He was reading a very thick ancient book with glasses perched on his nose. I felt it was rude of him to not even look up to acknowledge our presence.

When Anne said "Hello Abner" Abner startled a bit and said "Hello both of you, I believe you are a bit early" he said, eyeing the clock which showed 8:20 pm.

"Have a seat, we'll start as soon as Cara and Bryan arrive. As you see my friends and I have delved and scrutinized on every single detail which could probably help you in your quest".

Exactly five minutes later Cara arrived and on seeing me and Anne already seated she thought she was late and apologized. Abner said "Cara why do you apologize? No apologies are required for coming early, I was expecting everyone at around 8:30 and you showed up five minutes early".

Looking around Cara asked Abner "Where is Bryan?".

Abner rolled his eyes and said "Do you think Bryan will ever come on time?".

Time passed and I only got even more bored as every second passed. Thirty minutes later, when the clock ticked to 9:00 we saw Bryan arrive. He opened the door, sat on the chair and propped his legs on top of the table acting as if nothing had happened.

Seeing this Cara lost her temper "Bryan you should apologize for coming late".

Bryan who seemed to be confused "Why me? I am perfectly on time, after all, Abner told me the meeting was after dinner and I just finished having my dinner".

I thought, what Bryan said made perfect sense, Abner had never mentioned of any specific time.

So I commented, "Good point". To which Bryan gave me a high five.

Abner who didn't want to waste another second said "Please let's hurry up and get the meeting started and Bryan put your legs down there are books over here; please show some respect."

Now Bryan got a bit agitated but nevertheless put his legs down.

"Anne and Jane please pay attention".

Both Anne and I became more alert and we nodded. So, then Abner continued

"Both of you, to start the quest, you need to travel to the place in Pacific ocean where the Mariana Trench lies, from there, basically you have to go to the underworld. Now, since there's very little time in our hands and we need to find Ellie fast, we'll need to travel using the shortest distance. Since L'Abri is situated everywhere that won't be an issue".

"Wait, what do you mean by everywhere?" I cut Abner.

"L'Abri travels around the globe looking for new Ultimates. According to which our L'Abri keeps shifting, although the shifting doesn't affect us. It's very similar to the revolution of the Earth around the sun if you look at it that way.

Anne asked, "But going to Hawaii will take a lot of time and we cannot afford to spend that much time".

"Don't worry, you'll be going along with our expert pilot James and I promise he won't take that much time".

"Both of you have to be careful in your quest as it won't be a piece of cake, but isn't impossible either, although his Presage will slow you down" warned Abner.

Anne then became slightly confused, asked, "How will we fight all of them?".

This time, even before Abner could answer, Bryan said, "You have to fight them off with your weapon, there's no short cut and don't worry about your weapons now".

Cara, who spoke after a while asked, "But Abner, how will they get inside the underworld?"

"Good question" replied Abner.

"To get inside you'll need to use a portal and to use the portal you'll need a locket". The locket will be given to you after your DNA test. Once you want to teleport to the underworld, you'll have to hold your locket and say

> *"Portal of home*
> *We all are*
> *One or none*
> *Please take us together*
> *To the... (underworld)"*

Our next job was to get the teleporting locket for which, we went into the chemistry lab, situated in the university. There they took our hair samples, blood tests, fingerprints, etc. After about ten minutes we got our lockets. It was in a triangular shape with fire on the top, a leaf to the bottom left and water droplet to the bottom right and in the center a beautiful pearl with a lightning bolt imprinted inside.

Now we were almost ready for the quest, we only needed our weapons. While Abner and Cara decided to wait at the university Bryan, Anne and I quickly headed towards rena.

Once we reached Bryan told us to pick the weapons we had chosen earlier. So I went ahead and picked up the sword, while Anne picked up the bow and arrow.

As we finished choosing our weapons Bryan took us straight to Sacre where we saw Cara and Abner already there. As we reached the top Abner eyed to Bryan, who nodded and said *"Arrived, here are two warriors for whom their weapon awaits"*.

Then all of a sudden colourful and bright mist filled the room moreover for the first time the box opened. It was a mesmerizing sight to see. In fact instead of Sacre's voice, this time a female voice spoke *"Warriors please show me your weapons"*.

So following her instructions, Anne and I held our weapons in our palms raising it high. Then the weapons were taken away from our hands by some invisible force. After a minute or so, a bright light filled the room, so bright that we had to squint to see.

Once the light dimmed down I saw that my sword more modified this time having fire flames around the blade.

The female voice said, *"Jane, your sword now is light, fast and has a tremendous amount of power, use it well only for the good of one and all"*.

Another minute or so passed until Anne's bow and arrow appeared, it had a build, like that of fierce water waves.

The female voice then said, *"Anne your bow and arrow is like your friend and follows your instructions, use it wisely"*. *"Your weapons are magical and will be hidden in your palms when in trouble, you can take it out yourselves and always remember to use it for a good purpose and never with any greed in your heart"*.

Next, I saw my sword get into my palm right next to my lightning bolt in the form of a fire flame. After the voice silenced, all colours went back into the box.

Anne and I looked around since as we didn't see Cara, Bryan or Abner we assumed that all of them must have gone down. As Anne and I reached the entrance of the University we saw Cara, Bran and Abner waiting for us there.

Before we bid everybody goodbye confused I asked "What happened to Sacre?. How did he suddenly become so colourful?".

To that Bryan started to laugh and replied "Jane that wasn't Sacre that was his maiden Enchantress whose last wish was to stay with Sacre forever. She is the one who makes our ordinary weapons extraordinary".

"Oh" was all I said. We went back to our houses bidding everyone good night in addition also thanking all three of them for all the help and the information. I then reached my house, changed my clothes and slept. As I slept I saw lots of black clouds all around me. It looked as if a storm was coming giving me an uneasy feeling.

When I opened my eyes on looking outside I saw that the sun hadn't risen yet, but since I felt fresh I decided to wake up anyways. Thinking of what to do without disturbing anybody I went straight to the fighting arena and started to practice with my new weapon. I did everything that Bryan had told me yesterday, trying to avoid any mistakes. Neither did I have a watch nor did I bother to look at the time, I continued doing practice until I lost my breath.

As I sat to wipe my sweat, suddenly I saw Bryan standing right in front me. I jumped in surprise feeling as though my heart was in my hand. Bryan was smiling and on seeing my reaction he only laughed and said "Hi Jane your up early today aren't you?".

Then I felt awkward or rather embarrassed and responded "Yeah".

Then Bryan said "I am impressed by your passion and determination, but you still need some corrections and I'll help you with that".

So Bryan and I practiced more while he taught me lots of tricks and tips to improve my game. He told me how to defend better, by putting more power on the sword along with which he also taught me how to be swifter in the attack. After we had finished, Bryan and I went for breakfast.

There I saw Anne with a couple of books in her hand. We finished breakfast fast as fast as we could and then Anne told me that she got some guide books and maps of Hawaii.

She also said that Abner had given her a huge book with loads of information that could help. While we got ready Cara told us that James would be our pilot and will be waiting for us behind the university where there was a mini airport at sharp 10:00 am, which was just fifteen minutes from now.

Cara also told us that she had already checked our backpacks once again, added a bottle of water, some fresh food and also gave us monnaie which was Ultimate's money. We packed our last minute knick knacks and we were ready to go. It was time to go and bid goodbye to Cara, Abner, Bryan, the tree nymphs and our housemates before heading towards the helipad. As we were about to board the jet with James, I went downstairs and thanked Bryan individually, for all the last minute tricks and tips and also for spending some time with me. He only smiled and gave me hug wishing me best of luck. As we boarded the jet, excitement crept all over me as I remembered the first time I had been on an airplane when I was just a little girl. I remember how we were so high above the ground and flying through the clouds. The jet started along with which we soared in the sky far, far away from L'Abri.

CHAPTER 6

OUT IN THE REAL WORLD

At first, we started going like any other ordinary jet when suddenly James exclaimed "Hold on!" and we took off at great speed, it almost seemed like we were going at the speed of light. I felt terrible along with which my stomach squeezed really bad. When I managed to look at Anne, I felt even worse as her face turned pale white as a consequence it looked like as if she were petrified.

After what seemed only like a few seconds, a mixture of black and gray scary ghost like figures started to cover the jet's windshield. Soon the whole jet became pitch black surrounded by the ghost like figures.

Anne asked "What are these things?".

James, who was now losing control of the jet, said "These are the Presage, they are his Presage. He knows of your coming, save yourselves, Jane and Anne!!".

Those were the last words I heard until I realized that the jet was spinning round and round really fast uncontrollably.

My breathing was raged and my head was pounding. There was no way of escaping this as we were bound to die. As my vision was getting blurred I closed my eyes. I still had my eyes shut not aware of what's happening around me until I heard this loud boom too loud in my ears after which things started to black out slowly.

Regaining my consciousness slowlyI opened my eyes, then I managed to get up and look around. I saw that the Presage had gone although our jet had broken down into a thousand pieces. I saw James coming towards me, he had a few bruises on his body and a slight burn on his arms. Then looking at myself I saw that nothing major had happened to me only a few cuts here and there with some blood oozing out.

Suddenly something occurred to me, if James and I were here, where was Anne?. Oh no! This can't be it. Without losing another second I started to look for Anne, James too joined in. Despite the fact that I searched everywhere repeatedly, I couldn't find Anne. Tears started to pour as hopelessness filled within. I had never ever felt so hopeless and helpless in life.

Forget about the underworld, forget about the quest, she meant the world to me furthermore, I wouldn't lose her for anything. This was so pathetic.

"Noooo!!" I screamed, hoping she would walk up to me. I looked at the people passing around, even though I screamed so much nobody helped or looked. James came and sat down next to me trying to comfort me saying "Don't worry nothing will happen to Anne".

I screamed, saying "So you think she's fine somewhere where I cannot even see her?".

My screaming, I realized, could make James angry, but instead he then calmly said "I understand how you feel Jane, but screaming won't help either. Although humans can see us, they can't see us during a quest or any of our weapons for their own safety. Also, nothing can harm Anne, our lightning bolt protects us. Or else how could we survive this horrible air crash. Get up Jane we need to keep looking, I know Anne is here".

I was happy with his determination which brought hope into my otherwise hopeless mind.

We started looking for Anne again. Dust filled the place along with which the setting sun made visibility very low. From the other side I heard James scream "Jane come here quick I found her".

I ran, I sprinted as fast as I could, jumping and dodging some of the jet pieces. There I saw Anne lying on one of the pieces of the jet, looking very pale. Tears rushed to my eyes, I never felt so happy in my entire life. As James scanned her he said that she was alive, although she was breathing extremely slowly. On hearing this all my happiness got washed away. As James moved away, trying to think, I was left stupefied.

James then said, "She's still alive, but life isn't guaranteed, unless she starts to breathe normally again. I think; maybe she got suffocated or something inside the jet".

So James pulled Anne out into fresh air. As I knew my best friend was probably taking her last few breaths, I went and hugged her. WhileI hugged her, I remembered all the happy moments we spent together, along with which my tears kept on flowing.

Suddenly I heard Anne say "Jane?" and I couldn't believe my ears, maybe just me imagining things, but then she opened her eyes and got up. I gave her a huge hug and squeezed her as hard as I could; as if I would lose her the next second. Anne was just as astonished as me. Then Anne asked "What happened and why are you hugging me so hard?". So I explained everything, then I looked at James who was only watched with a smile. He then called Anne over furthermore he also handed our backpacks which were, fortunately, safe.

"Now I shall leave and I wish all the best to both of you".

He then held onto his pendant muttered some words after that whoosh James disappeared into thin air. For a moment Anne and I just stood there flabbergasted. Then we took our backpacks and started walking around looking for a place to spend the night. As Anne and I wandered around looking for a place to stay, we realized how hungry we were. We spotted a nice park, where we sat down taking out our sandwiches.

As I finished my food I saw Anne reading some guidebook.

"Luckily we have reached Hawaii our destination" Anne said.

I hadn't even thought of where we were until Anne told me. As both of us finished eating, we found a reasonably good looking motel at the corner of the street where we decided to spend the night. As we entered the motel I asked the receptionist for a room in which we could spend the night likewise, she said room number nine was available.

I handed her the monnaie and waited for the change. While waiting I looked at Anne, who seemed to be stupefied, which made me ask her what had happened.

She said, "The monnaie that you gave it to her has turned into normal dollars as soon as you touched it".

I hadn't even realized that then thought maybe there is some magic in the hands of Ultimates. The receptionist handed the remaining monnaie back along with a polite thank you. Only then did, I notice something that Anne had also noticed, her tongue was snake like freaking both of us out completely. I thought was she a monster?. Or maybe it was some fancy trend going on now. Anyway, there was nothing we could do about it with nowhere else to go and having given the monnaie this was our best shot. Moreover, it was only for one night.

We entered the room and feeling too lazy to change we directly hit the bed. I saw Anne was completely tired hence was deep asleep as soon as her head touched the pillow. It took me some time to fall asleep thinking about all what happened since the morning, especially to Anne and above all was glad to have her back. I was asleep for quite some time until I heard some noises, some noises that definitely didn't belong to this place.

I woke up with a start and saw Anne up right beside me. The Presage came towards us at high speed and just like the previous encounter we had with them even this time they outnumbered us. As if in reflex action I immediately took my sword out. As the Presage came charging towards us, I saw Anne was frozen in fear, I knew I had to do something or else everything would be finished. I quickly zoomed towards the Presage cutting through them, just in the nick of time to save me and Anne from any damage.

Seeing me attacking Anne also mustered courage as a consequence took out her weapon. We started cutting through as well as shooting at all the Presage which surrounded us. Under relentless fury of our attack the Presage started to disintegrate one by one. We fought our way out of the door. Anne and I ran out of the door as fast as our legs could carry us, along with which even the Presage followed us.

They were screaming "mort mort" "jamais jamais" and I had no idea what that meant. Anne and I kept on running, we continued running and stopped only when noises had trailed off. Anne and I both were damn tired, so we sat down on the sand soon realizing that the sea was close by. As I caught my breath I saw Anne taking out a map only then did I realize I had left my backpack at the motel.

Looking at me Anne said "That was one horrible and frightening night" to whichI commented "Freaking motel".

We remained silent for a while the only sound being that of our footsteps as we watched the sunrise.

Breaking the silence I asked "Anne, do you know where we are going?"

"Yes, of course, we are headed to the bus stop" Anne said confidently while still looking at the map in her hand

"We'll take the bus to get to the pacific ocean" furthermore she added.

I just kept following Anne although when we finally reached the bus stop, we didn't really find any bus, instead we found only one cab as if it was waiting for us.

The cab driver pulled his window down and said "Hi Jane and Anne hop on".

In spite of yesterday's events I hopped into the car without any hesitation, however Anne thought twice and eventually came in. The cab driver introduced himself "I am John Winsten and you are on your way to the pacific ocean".

He then passed us some gum saying "Relax ladies" in a perfect British accent.

"I am from L'Abri and I have been waiting for you guys so y'all can chill out," he continued.

Although Anne and I both politely refused the gum ; we were at ease since he looked normal and didn't have a snake like tongue,. Unexpectedly at an instance the cab picked up speed, Anne and I screamed and all I managed to say was holy! Until boom! We reached the pacific ocean.

"You guys reached here in exactly 1.895 seconds to be very precise" John Winsten said with pride in his voice Anne and I thanked him offering some monnaie but he refused to take any as he said it was his job. John Winsten then zoomed off in his cab, leaving us dazed in front of thehuge water body.

Not knowing what to do, I started to scream for help; unfortunately there was no one. "Jane don't be stupid, shut up, there is no one here, instead try to think of what to do".

Since nothing striked me I started to walk in circles while Anne did the thinking part.

Soon Anne exclaimed "Oh my god!. How could we have been so dumb?".

Anne, who seemed to be super excited said "Jane hold the water with one hand while your pendant with the other

hand. Then say the portal thing Abner had told us before
On the count of three two one and together we said

We all are
One or none
Please take us together
To the underworld

Just after saying the portal rhyme it seemed like the world
was swirling around us, what is more, is that my head was
also spinning uncontrollably until I heard a soft thud.
As I got up and tried to look around I couldn't identify
anything as it was pitch dark moreover something smelled
awful about this place. As my eyes started to adjust slowly I
realized mustiness filled the room and while I looked behind
I saw Anne who looked terrified.

I knew exactly why she was terrified moreover she was
terrified for a good reason. I could hear the familiar voice of
the Presage coming towards us saying "mort mort" "jamais
jamais" however this time things were even worse. They
appeared to be darker, larger along with which Anne said she
could see blood in their mouth. Out numbering us as always
the Presage had already surrounded us in all directions.
Without any further ado, we immediately took out our
weapons as they started to get closer.

While Anne started to shoot the arrows I started to use my
sword at the Presage but to our vain nothing happened, they
only became more powerful with every attack we made and
the bad thing was we were losing our energy.

Anne who was starting to feel exhausted said "This is never going to work out".

Then I remembered something that Bryan had told me during practice. He had mentioned about a weak spot that every opponent has.

I told this to Anne, she immediately said, "What about hitting the center?".

So Anne and I started to attack at the center of the Presage. One by one they started to disintegrate with blast of what seemed to be gray ash and soon both of us killed all the Presage.

Anne then closed her eyes and I was wondering what she was doing until I saw a beautiful garland around Anne's neck.

"Oh dear garland will you please show us the way to Ellie".

Just after saying this all the flowers in the garland fell down and a golden sparkle appeared Anne said "This will lead us to Ellie follow it".

We ran fast hoping not to lose track of the sparkle. We took sharp turns lefts and right in the dingy and dark underworld. We kept on following the sparkle ignoring the pain in our legs. It felt interminable when we finally bumped into something hard and the golden sparkle disappeared.

CHAPTER 7

THE HIM

Anne then put her finger on my lips saying "Listen carefully", so as I tried to listen hard I heard a soft noise coming from the thing we bumped into. It took me some time but then I realized that it was a cage.

I then heard a soft cry while Anne gently whispered "Ellie?".

As a reply, someone from within the cage screamed "Go away! Or eat me up, kill me!".

This definitely couldn't be Ellie her gentle voice couldn't have such madness. Then there were another series of tears when Anne just said "L'Abri".

I then heard something move from within the cage as well as something from behind our backs. Becoming alert I took my weapon out immediately. Then something turned inside the cage and without doubt it was Ellie although with eyes bloodshot and nose red due to constant crying, making her look gaunt and groggy. Anne and I at once tried to free her. We tried really hard, but the cage wouldn't budge.

I even tried using my sword when all of a sudden a very deep voice haunted from within said "No use".

I immediately spun around and froze to what I saw; something that creeped me out like never before. The thing I saw in front of me was practically all my worst nightmares put together to form something very bizarre. He was bald with veins showing all over his bald head, his eyes were blood red, his hands were like a mechanical machine. His back had spikes while his legs looked like normal legs and his teeth and mouth had blood smeared all over, but the worst part was he was green in colour cover with scales from top to bottom.

"I've been waiting for you Anne yet you never showed up so I thought why not bring you here and I knew you would come. However, I never knew you would make it this far alive moreover you surprise me by not even losing any of your body parts". Even his voice was something you wouldn't want to hear; devoid of any feeling. Becoming furious I screamed right on his face saying

"You're a big coward to hide in this place furthermore get us here because you're too scared to get out, aren't you?".

At once, he reacted to what I had said throwing a big white, mystical ball right at my face. Wow and I always thought that black was evil while white represented good and purity; clearly, the opposite happened here. Although I was petrified I knew I had to do something after coming all the way here, I wouldn't lose so easily. So I ducked using my sword for protection just the way Bryan had taught me. I dodged the powerful mystical ball at the nick of time. I got ready for more just in case he fired more.

Instead he didn't do anything but in a rather calm voice said "Since I know that both of you are my future meal anyways, I would want you to know who I am. I am Mal simply meaning evil". He continued to ramble some more like how he would conquer and stuff but clearly we zoned out. Ellie quickly took the opportunity and whispered "You can only defeat him by using your inner magic".

Then Anne asked "what about Sacre…"

"No time we have to do it at the same time to unite our powers and to use your inner magic think of someone or something you love the most and exert all your energy" Ellie explained in a hurry

"On the count of three! Two!…

I tried to focus hard on the thing I love the most when my loving and caring mom and dad appeared smiling at me always feeling proud of me.

Just as Ellie said three with all my energy, every bit of it. I put my palms and arm forwards making it look like I was pushing something. Then I expelled something from my palm with an immense amount of power.

I then saw the fire has been released from my palms and from the corner of my eye, I managed to see Anne had released water while Ellie had released a series of branches, leaves and roots. A loud roar filled the room while an extremely bright light was produced for which I had to shield my eyes.

At that moment all I could hear was a "Noo!!!".

As soon as the light was gone making the area dark again, I saw Ellie fall to the ground too drained and too tired. All she managed to say was take me home. I was myself extremely tired, but we hadn't finished yet, at least not until we reached L'Abri. Without warning, all the walls started to shake making cracks all around, giving us the sign that they were all going to break.

We had to do something fast and I told Anne to think of something quick. Anne was deep in thought with eyes closed as I held Ellie. I noticed that the place was breaking down in high speed as one pillar fell right behind us. In a panicked voice I told Anne that time was running out. Anne then opened her eyes and said "Jane hold on to Ellie tight and the pendant and sing the portal song again. Together on the count of three two one Anne and I said

> "Portal of home
> We all are
> One or none
> Please take us together
> Back to L'Abri"

I again got the swirling feeling, although this time it was only worse, firstly holding on to Ellie, secondly a piercing pain shot straight into my head, making me almost lose grip on Ellie. The pain in my head only got worse as the spinning feeling got faster. This portal took longer than the first tie we tried it. Then we finally reached L'Abri when I couldn't take it anymore. Even though I was so tired as soon as I landed at L'Abri, I got the feeling of elation within me. Anne and I had finally completed the quest which once I thought was impossible.

As we landed Bryan, Abner and Cara and lots of the other Ultimates gathered around us. Cara immediately took action. She took Ellie from my hands, which was a relief and said

"Well done both of you and congratulations. You look dead tired, so go have some rest".

Rest was the best word I heard in days. Too tired to change or wash my face I just landed on the bed and without a word and I fell asleep.

I woke up starving realizing that it had been long since I had any food. As I got up I saw Bryan, who gave me a bear sized hug and I was definitely glad to hold on while he also told me I had done a wonderful job. In fact he also said that I was in bed for two whole days, which actually surprised me. Then I told Bryan everything about the quest like as if he was an old friend of mine who listened to every bit of it happily. After I was done, he said he was very proud me for using his tricks wisely which made me super happy.

Then we made our way towards the cafeteria where I saw Anne, Cara and Abner seated while Anne was eating. I saw Anne having scrambled eggs and I too asked for one. As we ate Cara, Abner and Bryan said we had done an extremely good job.

Cara then said "We have a special gift for both of you and your bravery". She handed us beautiful looking bracelets having pearls and each of which had a lightning bolt. While the first pearl shined violet the rest of them remained white. Anne and I were both mesmerized by the bracelet.

"It's beautiful" Anne exclaimed.

Curious I asked why only one pearl shined violet.

Then Bryan answered "Ultimates who don't have this bracelet are called beginners. While Ultimates who finish their first quest are called intermediates; Ultimates who finish over seven quests are said to be in the advanced stage. They are then given the responsibility to take care of home".

To that Anne asked "So all three of you are in the advanced stage?".

"Yes," replied Bryan "All three of us, Ellie and all our previous headmasters".

Then Anne asked "Is there any possibility to get back the thing that you would have lost in the quest?".

Abner then asked "Why? Lost something important?. The monnaie is added to the bank maximum you would have only lost some food and clothes". Anne who was hesitant said "No nothing, just asking".

I knew she would have lost something important and asked "Anne please tell us what's wrong?".

Cara who hadn't spoken for a while said "Yes, of course, Anne don't be shy tell us".

Anne then almost in tears, choked "I am really sorry Abner I lost the ancient book that you had given to me".

Abner, who smiled instead of being disappointed said "Well, that was an important book, but not as important as your quest and saving Ellie".

Anne, who was still sad didn't say anything when to all of our surprises Abner gave Anne the exact ancient book in fact this one was even better as it was the latest version. Anne, who was flabbergasted screamed in joy and Abner just smiled saying "Now keep this one safe".

Anne thanked Abner a billion times and was so happy in fact even I was so happy seeing her. I then asked them, "You know, while coming back from the underworld directly to L'Abri I felt a piercing pain in my head".

Abner said that happens because our lightning bolt cannot hold that much power as it isn't a teleporter as a consequence doesn't work for long distance. You should have said take me back up and then from there come back to L'Abri probably by a flight or so.

Although at that moment what you did was the best because Ellie's condition was getting worse every minute".

Anne then asked if Ellie was better now, but Cara's expressions became serious and she said "Things weren't good while both of you were at rest".

I noticed that Cara looked slightly pale maybe agonizing for Ellie too much. Cara also said that Ellie hadn't shown any movement furthermore her body is getting colder slowly. The nurses and the doctors too couldn't find a way out. Even the tree nymphs tried but it was of not much help. So every day we would take turns keeping a close watch on Ellie and report if anything different happened. Days passed, but Ellie didn't show any movement. Five days went by, a week went by, nine days went by, then finally on the tenth day while Cara was watching, Ellie showed some movement immediately everyone was called. Ellie suddenly shot her eyes open and all she said was "Every thing's going to change and he'll rise stronger than ever".

PART 2

CHAPTER 8

SUSPICION IN THE AIR

Silence filled the room as I tried to think about what Ellie had just said. I couldn't find any meaning to it so as I looked around I noticed Abner with eyes closed deep in thought. The silence was broken when Ellie tried to weakly get up, people rushed to her aid. Ellie then finally got up and now fully in her senses said "That was the most horrifying experience ever and thank you Jane and Anne. I've no words to express how grateful I am".

Then both Anne and I said "No problem and welcome".

Everything seemed to be normal until, Ellie stared Anne, for a split second rather sternly. To which Anne looked as confused as I was.

Bryan, who had been quiet for a while asked "Ellie how did you disappear all of a sudden?". Curiosity started to rise as we all waited for an answer. Then Ellie giving a sigh said "Well, that's something I've been thinking of as well. I don't remember anything as if I was in a state of coma. It feels like some part of my memory has been erased, I only have blurred visions here and there. But I do remember something...".

"What? we all asked in unison.

Then Ellie with a serious tone said *"It was someone from inside"*.

Everyone was shocked and scared all at once filling the room with an awkward silence. Everyone's eyes shifted from one another. Then a small kid, who looked around thirteen said "I think it's either Jane or Anne".

My temper immediately shot up, who the hell does this kid thinks he is?. As I got ready to yell at him, Ellie stopped me and said "There's no point in randomly blaming others".

Cara, who was beside Ellie all this while said "I think Ellie needs some more rest before she can fully recover", so without another word all of us made our way towards the door.

As soon as I was outside I went towards that kid and said "Hey, you!"

then I felt someone tap me on my shoulders. I turned to see who it was and saw Bryan, who just looked at me, a signal not to say any word.

Heeding to Bryan's signal, I said, "Never mind" to that kid who was glad to get away.

Bryan then knowing what I would ask said "You know there's no point in messing up with a kid who's so young, you'll only end up losing your energy".

"Yeah" was all I said, knowing Bryan was right.

As we walked I casually asked "Bryan we finished Mal in the quest using our inner magic, right?. How is he going to be stronger?".

Bryan then replied "Jane you never really saw his ashes or him actually dying did you?. Moreover Ellie seemed pretty serious, also visions are a very important thing they aren't the same thing as dreams. You never know how much they can sometimes affect a person".

I didn't say anything to that and we continued walking.

"Bryan if I hadn't dodged the mystical ball Mal had released would I have died?".

Bryan didn't say anything in at first but just looked at me. His eyes suddenly looked lost and for the first time I would have actually said he did look a little sad.

"Well, Jane it depends on the mystical ball. The intensity of it, where it hits us as well as if we are capable of bearing the pain. It usually causes a burning sensation to the skin and leaves bruises at the least."

I just looked at Bryan and kept quiet when Bryan suddenly said "Moreover who says mystical ball?, it's called Fonce. Although Fonce means dark we use it because magic isn't ordinary and can lead to dark things if not used wisely".

"Oh okay" was what I said while Bryan quickly added "Keep along with the time's kid" giving me a sideways smirk.

"Hey in my defense I just got here!" I said.

"Says the person who has already finished a quest and been here for way more than just a week or a day".

"Whatever" I said sticking my tongue out.

Once we reached our house Bryan said "Come on, I'll get you your clothes". I remember the first time I came L'Abri I had seen Ultimates wear different clothes but then I never paid close attention. Now that I saw closely I noticed everyone wore black jeans or shorts, sneaker or running shoes and different coloured T-shirts mainly different shades of reds, blues and greens. This was different from black T-shirts, blue jeans and running shoes which Anne and I were wearing. It was sort of odd how I hadn't noticed all of this earlier. Bryan handed me some fresh clothes saying "Jane now you are officially an Ultimate!".

I quickly changed and the clothes fit perfectly. Now I wore an orange T-shirt with red flames at the bottom, a pair black jeans and new running shoes.

I came out and Bryan said "Now young lady, you look stunning".

I looked at Bryan with a smile hoping that I wasn't blushing. It was dark already and time for dinner. Dinner was a silent affair with no one knowing what to say. We finished eating quickly after which all of us headed towards our houses.

I wasn't that tired and I waited for my eyes to feel heavy. I gave a thought to what Ellie had said which gave rise to many questions. Was he really going to rise again? Was everything actually going to change? These questions really bothered me. Or was Ellie just having visions?. Maybe that kid was right about Anne or me harming Ellie, though not intentionally but maybe without knowing. Maybe he's controlling someone. There were so many possibilities and so many "may be". I knew I had to tell this to Anne, Cara or Ellie, maybe even Bryan or Abner.

I sat up straight for a while, still waiting for sleep. Then all of a sudden I heard soft footsteps which alarmed me; immediately I got my sword out. The footsteps came closer when put of the blue a head popped up in my bunk.

I was about to swing my sword until I heard a voice that said "Relax Jane it's only me".

I immediately recognized the voice and withdrew my sword, it was Bryan.

Relieved, I let him into my bunk.

"Holy cow!. You would have killed me by now if I hadn't told you it was me" said Bryan.

I laughed and asked "What are you doing here?"

To which Bryan replied "How come you haven't slept yet?".

I was really tempted to tell him about my thoughts, but decided to tell him later.

So instead I said "I am not getting sleep, just kept thinking about what Ellie said".

"Relax Jane, what are you? Malin?" Bryan asked.

"No," I replied

He said "Get some sleep I'll wake you up before dawn, we need to start practicing again".

"Okay".

Kissing me on my forehead he went down.

Anne was already sound asleep until a piercing pain shot inside her head, she immediately sat straight clutching her head. As the pain reduced Anne again tried to sleep, but then a voice spoke to her. "So Anne how did you like that?". In no time she recognized the voice it was Mal. Anne then said "Go away!".

"Go away? I'm already in..."

"Where?" Anne asked, but the voice had already trailed off.

It only felt like I had slept for an hour or so until Bryan's voice woke me up. I got up, washed my face changed and followed Bryan outside in the dark. First Bryan and I decided to jog aroundL'Abri. I usually did go for jogging back in New York, however this time I felt tired and had to stop. Bryan looked at me not very pleased saying "You've to increase your stamina Jane".

We then went to the fighting arena where I had some water and wiped my sweat.

Bryan then said "Jane listen, I've seen that you are a good fighter moreover you also grasp things faster than most people yet you are still behind the group. Today will be your first fight".

This one got me nervous. "Today we'll focus on fighting with bare hands" Bryan said.

He taught me punches, kicks afterward he taught me how to go for the neck. We did around 10 reps for each of tactics and after an hour or so we finished. We went to our house, immediately got into the shower after which we headed for breakfast.

Bryan said "I have to train the rest, so see me around the noon". I immediately knew this meant I could talk to Anne. After breakfast, I met Anne. I told her everything about my thoughts of yesterday night only leaving the Bryan part.

Anne then said that she also had a bizarre dream about Mal already being here.

"Jane we ought to tell this to one of them, maybe Cara because Abner is busy with some research".

"Bryan too, took everyone for training moreover Cara could also be busy with the Soins Ultimates. So how about Ellie?" I suggested.

Anne agreed and we headed towards Ellie's office. As we opened the door we saw Ellie seated behind her table once again. On seeing us Ellie said "Hello Jane and Anne have a seat".

So then Anne and I took turns and told her about my thoughts and Anne's dream. Ellie with deep concern said "If he's actually here, then things can get worse any minute. We should meet up in the auditorium".

We left the office and Anne bid me goodbye as she had some work at the library. There was still some time till I could meet Bryan so I decided to go for another jog wanting to improve my stamina. I followed the same track Bryan and I took starting from our house going to the fighting arena, then the office and entering the outskirts of the forest going behind the university touching the airport and coming back. I finished one nonetheless this time I didn't stop and went for another round. Today was going to be my first match certainly I didn't want to screw things up. After the second round, I directly headed towards the cafeteria.

I finished lunch and looked around for Bryan, who immediately caught my eyes and told me to go towards the fighting arena. I went to the fighting arena and in no time Bryan had arrived. Then Bryan said "Now we'll focus on defense".

We practiced with Bryan only hit harder as every second passed. My arms and body were begging for rest when Bryan finally called the break. I immediately lay down flat on the ground. Seeing me Bryan smiled and looking up, I smiled too. He gave me his hand and pulled me up. Then he asked "Jane now you decide what kind of a player you want to be, offense or defense?".

"Offense" I said without any hesitations.

First of all, I found offense to be more fun. Secondly, I didn't have the patience to wait for my opponent to make the first move.

After my answer, Bryan said "Very well then, the matches will start after an hour".

I went straight to the house too exhausted and tired. As I laid on my bed I tried to build a strategy for the oncoming fight. I first visualized a punch, kick and block sequence, then thought kick, punch and block sequence would be better.

"Oh, this is so annoying," I said to myself.

So instead I just took deep breaths trying to relax. Within minutes I was fast asleep, when I got up I saw Bryan come towards me. Soon he was on my bunk "Thought of something?" he asked.

"Yeah, I tried thinking of something, but... well, I screwed it up" I replied not very happy about it.

"Jane having power isn't the only thing, you also need to be fast, accurate and smart. So here's the strategy for you, go on the offensive right at the beginning in the process keep looking for places where your opponent's defense isn't strong. Look at the opponent's eyes apart from offense always be ready to defend just in case"

Keeping Bryan's tips in mind, I went in to get ready. When I reached the arena not many people had arrived, although within minutes the fighting arena was crowded. The matches had been announced and to my surprise my match was first.

I went in the ring and my opponent looked brutal. She was a girl of about my age named Lary. On the count of three, two, one, the match started. I immediately got ready releasing a punch right at her face. She defended the punch well while I got ready for defense in case she charged. Seeing that she didn't charge I charged back. I noticed that she didn't block the area around her ribs and kicked twice nonstop. She let a groan and without wasting any time I moved to the side, got her neck pushing her to the ground. I was on top of her ready to punch her face when Bryan said "Stop! Jane wins".

I was extremely happy, especially since I won my first match. Although I knew I had to compete with tougher opponents in the coming rounds. I went towards the right while Lary went left, both of us following Bryan's instruction. The second match was between two guys. Their match was fierce furthermore it lasted much longer than ours. The match ended and one of the guys joined me. He then said "New here, huh?".

"Came recently," I replied.

"My name is Kevin" he said and shook my hand.

"Jane".

I looked at him for a split second noticing that he had jet black hair and his eyes were darker than his hair.

The matches went on and on. After what felt like quite a while my name was called this meant that I had to fight again. Startled, I got up. I walked to the ring and in front of me, I saw Kevin. I knew this guy was a really good fighter moreover his offense was exceptionally strong as well.

On the count of three two one and I went for his neck. Instead of defending his neck, he punched me hard in my core. I moved back almost losing balance. I then went for a kick which he blocked with ease. Kevin then went straight for my face, throwing a punch. I was able to block that, but then he instantly went for my nose. My nose hurt likewise for a moment I saw everything blurred. Getting mad and wanting revenge I kicked hard on his stomach He was definitely surprised and taking that opportunity I went for his neck and he too came at my neck. I thought I could knock him off, but he was way too strong and with a tremendous blow he knocked me down, I was flat on the ground.

"Match over, Kevin wins" I heard Bryan say.

I was still on the ground when Kevin looked down and said "Good match Jane". I got up and realized our match was the last as I saw all the Ultimates make their way to the door. I got out of the ring and sat down on the bench in the corner of the fighting arena. Bryan came and sat down next to me handing me a towel. My nose stopped bleeding sooner than I thought it would. After a long silence Bryan said "Jane you played pretty well, exceeded my expectations".

"Yeah, wonder why I lost," I said in a very dull voice.

Bryan then said "Winning isn't the only thing. Doing your best and being happy after that is what matters.

I didn't say anything to that although a small smile crept on my face. After a while, both of us went towards the cafeteria.

While I was totally out of breath things weren't easy for Anne either. Anne had her first IQ test at the University where she was having a tough time competing with another Ultimate named Will. Anne was aiming for a better IQ than Will, but Will seemed to be unbeatable.

We had dinner along with an announcement about which I and Anne had been already aware of. After dinner, everybody made their way towards the auditorium as instructed by Ellie As we all reached the auditorium we saw Ellie, Cara, Bryan and Abner stood on stage. Then Ellie said "Since we all know that evil lures are getting closer by the minute, I've decided that we must start another quest".

To which there was a round of applause. Ellie continued saying "There should be exactly five members who will go on the quest. Two from Audacieux, two from Malin and one from Soins".

Then Cara said "From Soins I nominate Lacey". Cheers filled the room as Lacey went towards the stage. Lacey who was really happy had dirty blonde hair which was straight, very fair skin accompanied with beautiful hazel eyes.

Bryan then said "From Audacieux I nominate Kevin and…" Utter silence filled the room as everyone crossed their fingers.

"It ought to be Jane" Bryan said.

I was so… I mean out of everyone, Bryan nominated me and I felt like I was the world's happiest person. With a huge smile on my face, I made my way towards the stage. Then Abner said "From Malin I select two of my best Ultimates proving themselves worthy of. Will and Anne".

I was even happier when Anne was chosen. Then I looked at Will who I hadn't seen before. He had beautiful golden blonde hair with forest green eyes. We were now five Ultimates all ready to go on a quest.

CHAPTER 9

A SHOCK

Ellie then dispersed the rest of the Ultimates while the five of us followed Ellie along with Cara, Bryan and Abner. When we reached Ellie's office, Anne and I explained everyone about what I thought and about Anne's dream. After we finished Bryan was the first to say something. "Since Anne said Mal already in, we better start things fast before he can start to destroy L'Abri or harm any of us".

Then I asked Ellie "So any time any of his Presage can enter the home?

Before Ellie could answer Abner said "No, that isn't possible because our lightning bolt protects us and our home".

Not having much information we all knew where to go. As we reached the attic Ellie said "Sacre we have come here to seek your guidance for our new quest".

Tele mist filled the room as a result we heard Sacre's voice. "Things aren't good and they are bound to get worse. With an army much bigger than ever Mal comes. He comes mightier and more powerful. He lies where he always was, fortunately, he hasn't reached yet. All I can say is hope, love and above all care for one another; let hatred and jealousy never conquer you..."

This time Sacre didn't give much of a solution just some wise words I would say. All I understood was that our quest was going to be much harder this time. The mist started to disappear back into the ruby and just as we were about to go down unexpectedly Anne fell down. The strange part was that Sacre came out without being called saying "All of you back away!" in an alarming tone. Everyone backed away, but I went towards Anne, who just lay there on the ground motionless.

I took another step forward but something held my hand turning around Isaw Bryan. I thought I could still reach for Anne but with just one jerk Bryan pulled me back. Tears started to flow before as I saw Anne's eyes glow white and her skin turn pale. Bright white mist started to swirl around Anne, in addition the white mist started to speak just like Sacre, though haunted within saying "I am back and I shall destroy each one of you slowly. Prepare to face my wrath. Bwahhahaha!".

Anne got up looking normal, maybe not aware of anything. All of us looked at one another and decided not to tell Anne anything about what had just happened. So silently we went our way down. I reached my house and lay on my bunk burying my face in the pillow not being able to control the continuous tears. I couldn't believe what had just happened.

Anne was the one who Mal was using. Manipulating her making her do wrong things and Anne was the one who kept on giving the information to Mal. It was way too much for me to believe. What was worse was that all I could do was cry and in no way help her out of this.

Another series of tears rushed when I felt a gentle tap on my back. With my eyes probably swollen and red I saw Bryan. I didn't want to him see me in this way so I turned away I thought he would say I looked pathetic or ask why I was crying instead he hugged me.

He then whispered in my ear "Jane, I'm sorry for what happened there, but you need to brave and strong. Don't just sit here and blame yourself. You need to be a fighter and fight Mal for what he did to your friend. Moreover, Jane you can't be sure if he is completely controlling Anne yet".

Bryan had a point furthermore now determination replaced the anger that I had before. Bryan was right, he was always right. I felt much better now and the tears stopped.

He then kissed me. For a minute I just froze not knowing what to do and not expecting that either. After what felt like a second, I closed my eyes and kissed him back instantly wrapping my arms around his neck. After we broke apart I just looked at him and smiled. It didn't feel like the fairy tales that I read about in books. I didn't feel any sparks or see any shooting stars instead it was simple and sweet. And to be honest there was nothing more that I would ask for.

Bryan then said "Tomorrow morning, so sleep fast".

I smiled at how he changed the topic all of a sudden. He smiled and went away. My head was about to touch the pillow when Bryan suddenly came back up again.

"What happened?" Without responding he kissed my forehead after which he went down. I wondered how my mood changed all of a sudden like as if Bryan had magic.

I woke up slightly earlier than dawn and saw Bryan was already ready. I quickly freshened up and changed. Although we went for a jog again and took the same route we were faster than yesterday, in fact we hit another round one as well. After the third round I was completely exhausted and sat on the bench.

"Hmm, not bad, the improvement is shown" Bryan said who seemed to be impressed.

"Thank you".

After a few minutes we got up; did a few warm up exercersises after which Bryan said "Today we'll focus more on the sword as you'll likely use your sword more than bare hands. We better hurry up as we don't have much time in fact you'll start in the quest right away".

"Woah! What the hell?" I said with astonishment in my voice

"There's less time Jane..." was all that Bryan said.

I picked up a sword from the arena when Bryan said "Not with those swords," and asked me to use my own sword which was embedded within me. So I closed my eyes and imagined my sword come out from my fire symbol. Once I opened my eyes there it was, in my hand.

Without wasting any time we started to practice. The practice was hard moreover, Bryan also played much tougher than before. I had to play fast as well as apply a lot of energy. We continued with a series of offensive and defensive slides. I almost gave up, becoming really tired and at this juncture Bryan cut me on my left arm.

"AAH!" I cried and at that instance I knew I had to get him. Mustering all my strength I sprang into the air and took my sword to Bryan's neck. Though taken by surprise, Bryan also reacted quickly going for my neck. Now both of us had our swords at each other's neck

"Now in situations like this, when you are damn tired, you need to be smart, as you know you cannot defeat your opponent by force".

To this, I was kind of offended because the events of the day had drained me otherwise I wasn't that weak after all. Although in a way he was right. Last time I had faced a position like this was with Kevin who knocked me off in just one blow. Not having another option I listened to Bryan.

"You should use your body weight with the help of your head, go for the stomach and then slash your opponent with your sword.".

I liked this idea a lot and we practiced this move for some time. Bryan finally called a break when my energy and stamina levels screamed zero percent. After having getting rid of our sweaty clothes in the shower we headed towards the cafeteria.

Breakfast tasted much better today after the tiring training and while I indulged myself in the food I looked for Anne althoughI couldn't find her. After feeling better with some rest I went to Cara. I found her near the Soins bench along with Lacey. I saw that they were already getting the backpacks, monnaie and food packed up.

On seeing me Cara said "Jane, I'm glad you're here. Can you please get Kevin, Anne and Will? Thanks Jane"

Before I could even say yeah sure or something of that sort she was gone.

So first I decided to get Kevin as Anne was out of sight. I went to the house searched all the bunks, went to the fighting arena, still he was not to be seen anywhere. As I kept looking for Kevin I saw Anne come out of the forest. She looked much better than yesterday only with dirt covered all around her.

Before I could ask her anything she said "I went to the forest and helped the tree nymphs plant trees, we had a lot of fun".

Then I told her about the quest being in an hour or so likewise, her reaction was pretty predictable, as baffled as I was.

Anne then in a hurry said "Jane, I'll change and try to look for Will".

Anne went while I continued looking for Kevin. Despite the fact that I searched everywhere I was still not able to find him. So I decided to go back and let Cara know he wasn't anywhere.

I reached the Soins bench and said "Cara I couldn't find Kevin but Anne and Will are on the way".

And they sure were as I saw them get out of the Malin house.

"It's okayJane, Kevin will eventually know.

Soon after Anne and Will arrived.

Cara said "It would really help if you guys could arrange for a meeting now".

So Will went to get Abner, Anne decided to inform Ellie while I looked for Bryan. I started to make another round of L'Abri when I saw Bryan and Kevin come out of the university. I then told them about the meeting first after which I asked where they had gone.

Then Kevin said "I finally got my weapon fixed as it was not in full condition since it almost broke from the previous quest".

Bryan decided to go directly to Ellie's office while Kevin and I went the Soins bench. Cara handed both us our backpacks and then Abner, Lacey, Cara, Anne, Will, Kevin and I went to Ellie's office.

We settled as fast as we could knowing that time was running out of our hands. Ellie started by saying "We've all gathered here to sum all the information we have on the quest

Abner then continued saying "Since Jame's helicopter hasn't been repaired yet, all of you shall be travelling by bus reaching the pacific ocean consequently then using the portal to reach the underworld".

"All of you have hope, love and care for one another". "Stay together at all times and don't split up" added Cara.

Then Bryan said "Since this time he's stronger than ever all of you will always have to be alert keeping your weapons at your fingertips".

Abner then said "We know he's powerful but always remember brain over brawn. Furthermore, he's a very cunning and shrewd man so never listen to him as it'll always be a trap".

Ellie then said "I know that all of you can do this. Give it your best shot. Also remember that all of you have magical powers within yourselves".

"I think it's time to go" Bryan said while Abner looked at the clock and nodded which said eleven.

Before any of us could get up I asked "Where's the exit?".

"The exit to L'Abri is a magical boundary which keeps us invisible from the outsiders, as of now we are going towards the helipad" responded Ellie.

We reached the helipad soon enough however we continued to walk. We reached much further then the helipad, it looked like a barren piece of land which appeared never ending as we continued to walk. Kevin and Bryan were walking in front of us. We finally stopped after what felt like millions of years when Kevin said "Ouch!". Kevin moved back as if there was an invinsible wall while Ellie walked in front held her hand out and muttered something. After finishing saying those words she gestured us to walk in front. Kevin was the first one to go and just as he took another step forward he was gone. Woah! Where did Kevin go? Did he just vanish in thin air?. Will, Lacey and Anne went and disappeared just like Kevin. It was my turn and before getting in for the last time I looked in Bryan's eyes who mouthed the words "Be brave".

Chapter 10

Begins

I went through with my eyes closed and as I opened them, I saw Anne, Kevin, Will and Lacey looking at me. Then I realized they were not exactly looking at me, but they were looking at something behind me. I also turned expecting to see home, but instead I saw a huge forest. L'Abri just disappeared and I stared in awe.

We were surrounded by wilderness then Will said "I've been here before we just need to keep walking forward and then we'll hit the road and a bus will pass by sooner or later".

All of us followed Will and sure enough, we did end up hitting the road. We waited for a while after which a bus arrived. The driver looked crazy while the bus coach a lady with curly hair covering her face that her eyes wouldn't show. All five of us, took the last seat making ourselves comfortable. Actually, let me correct myself, we took the last seat because the front seats were occupied by passengers wearing black pants and dark hoods showing no movement at all. And that's why all of us took the last seat to stay as far from them

"Hold on guys I think I've been on this bus before," said Lacey

The bus unexpectedly started to go haywire, the driver was driving like a maniac. I suspected that the dude was crazy from the first time I saw him. The driver didn't slow down in fact he kept on increasing speed going through cars, just missing huge accidents. Anne then said, "Guys, I have never travelled at a normal speed in all the days I have spent at home".

Will then replied "This is how it is here Anne. You should get used to it".

"Yeah! We are extraordinary people with extraordinary speed. We are the Ultimates" Kevin said as if he was enjoying all of this.

As we were busy chatting about L'Abri and its extraordinary speed we didn't even notice that the crazy driver was standing in front of us. While I wondered who was driving the bus, in a reflex action I also took my sword out. Suddenly all the passengers with hoods, stood up while the bus coach stood beside the driver.

"What is happening, who the hell is driving the bus?" Will asked looking confused.

"We need to get out of here" Kevin said charging and taking his cue all of us also followed.

Seeing this the crazy driver charged at me knocking me off balance. Now he clung to me and the bus coach also tried to come at me, but Will kept her at bay, he was ready to attack if she took another step forward. While Anne and Kevin charged at the people with hoods Lacey on seeing me in trouble, pulled the crazy driver off me. I got up and stabbed the driver right at his heart. He staggered away with my sword still sticking in his body while blood was oozing from his wound.

Lacey started to panic saying "What should we do?".

"Leave" I said and ran up to the crazy bus driver pulling out my sword. Blood started to flow faster and he collapsed, the bus coach let out a loud scream after which even she was gone. We all went to the door and jumped out of the bus., Right after which the bus exploded. Fortunately, none of us were badly injured. Only a nick here or a cut there.

"What now?" Kevin asked.

"We have to keep moving". I said.

"Where to?, in which direction?" asked Lacey.

Anne then looked around trying to observe the surroundings. Will said "Looking at the roads and stores I think we are in Japan".

"Will is right moreover the inscriptions make things clear" Anne added.

"Out of all the places in the world… Japan" Lacey sighed.

"Those filthy spirits wanted to delay us," Kevin said.

"So…" I began,

then Lacey said "I think we should call Mr. Winsten I'm sure he'll help".

"Good idea Lacey, he is always nearby and waiting for our call, however the problem is I don't know how to call him?" Kevin said.

"Calling him just like how we call Sacre, won't hurt" Anne said.

Then all five of us together said "Mr. Winsten we all need your taxi. Can you please help?". We waited but only the leaves blew with no answer.

"If you would've noticed Mr. Winsten's weakness, he gets buttered rather easily, so putting some butter in our call may help" Will said.

With Will's new idea all of us this time said "Mr. Winsten we are waiting for your cab, the most fabulous and the fastest cab ever. Oh, and of course not forgetting that you are the best cab driver too".

Sooner than we expected, we heard a voice which said "Awww look at you sweeties I am on my... no wait, you are on my way, to come towards me listen with care.

> *Where aroma lures you and me*
> *There nature's beauty you'll see*
> *Come there and you'll find me*
> *With my Hiroshima you'll see"*

With that, Mr. Winsten's voice was gone.

Will then looked at us and smirked, saying "Look, I told you".

"So now we have the clues; we only need to solve them, which will eventually lead us to Mr. Winsten." Lary said with excitement in her voice.

"Okay, let's get started!" Kevin said.

"Where aroma lures you and me" Lacey said.

"Hmm" Anne started to think.

"Aroma!? I'm hungry" I said. At that, all of us laughed.

"Jane! You're a genius" Will exclaimed.

"Over here Mr. Winsten is talking about food as he uses the words lures and aroma. This means a place to eat in, like a restaurant" Wil said confidently,

"Perfect! The first part is solved; now where nature's beauty you'll see" Anne said.

Kevin then said "By nature Mr. Winsten could mean flowers and trees. Maybe it's a garden or something".

"Nice thought Kevin" complemented Will.

"Thanks dude"

"You know what guys, wouldn't it be so perfect if there was a beautiful sunset along with the restraint that would be so romantic" Lacey said

"Hmm food and the sunset go perfectly" I commented which only made me more hungry.

"So now we have got two options a nice garden or a beautiful sunset" Will said.

"I think I'll go with the sunset as it seems to be more appropriate if you look up, almost time for dusk" Anne pointed out.

"Agreed so Mr. Winsten is in some restaurant with a good view of the sunset" I said finding sense in what Anne said.

Not bad so far. Now the third sentence says with my friend Hiroshima you'll see" Kevin said.

"Now how does that make any sense, how do we care about his friend?" I said.

"Well, you never know it could be a clue" Will said.

"Yeah Will is right, it could be a clue" Kevin added.

"Although knowing Mr. Winsten's nature, he could also be kidding" Lacey said.

There was silence for some time as all of us tried to crack the last clue.

"I think I know what the last clue means" Anne said breaking the silence.

"What?" we asked Anne in curiosity.

"Maybe Hiroshima could be a restaurant's name after all, Mr. Winsten didn't mention any name moreover there could be billions of restaurants with a sunset view".

As of now since Anne's conclusion made the most sense.

I said, "Let's just walk until we find any restaurant named Hiroshima".

As we were about to start walking Kevin asked "But in which direction should we go in?".

"Pay attention and don't ask silly questions Kevin, we have to go westwards if we are looking for the sunset" Lacey said.

Kevin then said "Nevermind" although his face which was filled with embarrassment made all of us laugh.

"Hey guys check this out I have a map in my pocket" Will said.

"I have just realized that we don't have our backpacks" Kevin said.

"Me too," I replied.

"Anyway guys according to this map Hiroshima's is straight ahead in the left corner".

We kept on walking ahead, hoping to see Hiroshima's in the left corner. And as soon as we spotted the restaurant we also spotted Mr. Winsten along with it sitting on the first bench. Mr. Winsten waved at us and asked us to sit down after which he ordered six bowls of chicken noodles.

As we waited for the order to arrive, Mr. Winsten said "So you guys finally made it. Good job. I thought I'll have to go and get y'all".

None of us said anything to that definitely feeling slightly offended at least. To be honest we weren't even that bad.

I then noticed a beautiful sunset through the window on the right hand side corner which immediately brought memories of mom and dad. When I was younger we would play along with the waves and make sand castles.

The noodles came and boy!, they smelled and looked good in fact they tasted even better. I then said "Hmm Japan is now my favourite place thank the Presage, we got some noodles"

Will said, "Mr. Winsten, though we felt offended by your words a few minutes ago, but your gesture to give us a treat and very kindly pay for it, has made us all extremely happy".

So all the brain cracking was worth the food we had. We all then hopped on to Mr. Winsten's cab, ready to go to the underworld, ready to fight. Ready to fight Mal.

As usual with an abnormally high speed we zoomed away and within no time we were right in front of the ocean.

"There you go. All the best guys" Mr. Winsten said and was gone.

This time I knew what to do and instead of screaming my lungs off, clutching on to our pendants all of us together said

> *"Portal of home*
> *We all are one or none*
> *Please take us together*
> *To the underworld.."*

I waited for the spinning feeling in my head. Although while waiting, I felt some kind of power pushing me backward. The power was way too strong thus losing my balance I fell down. Looking around I saw that everyone else had fallen down as well. We got up and said the portal of rhyme again.

Yet again we were pushed by the same strong invisible force. Now we were all desperate as to what should we do? We all sat down trying to think, on how to get into the underworld.

Then Will said "Guys I think we should go into the ocean and then say the portal rhyme".

Not having any other better idea I said "Okay, let's try it out,"

"Oh no my clothes will get wet!" Lacey wailed.

"Don't be silly Lacey. Obviously if your clothes will get wet if you get into the water unless you stay back here and cheerlead for us." Kevin said giving away a smirk.

Lacey who was bright red didn't say anything while all of us just laughed. Then we entered the water.

Once it was chin level Lacey asked "What now?".

"Let's say it again" Anne suggested and on the count of three two one we said the portal rhyme once again.

Well, unfortunately Will's idea wasn't any better.

While all of us felt helpless Lacey tried to bring a spark in us.

She said "Remember what Sacre said about having hope. I think that's all we need to have right now Also, when I was a kid, my mom always said I could do what I wanted to do if I believe in myself".

Kevin then said "Okay, one more time and this time lets imagine that we have reached the freaking underworld".

Three, two, one and holding on to our pendant we said the portal rhyme, determined to get inside.

Sure enough this time we finally made it as I got the spinning sensation. With that, we reached the underworld.

Chapter 11

We Meet Again

In no time I heard some familiar voices. Although it took me some time to recognize what they were saying. My sword was out as soon as I heard "jamais jamais mort mort". We drew our weapons out as the Presage came towards us. We attacked hard and within minutes they were disintegrated. We kept moving forward although being alert at the same time. Soon Presage attacked us forming a circle.

"We can all do this, come on man" Kevin said leading the fight.

We then saw more of them coming in not only were we outnumbered but we were out numbered by double or triple the number of Presage.

Then Kevin said "All of you run I'll handle them".

"We shouldn't split up," Lacey said, sounding worried, but too late Kevin was already gone. We kept moving, however I decided to turn around and help Kevin. Kevin saw me and smiled at first, but soon his smile turned into a scowl.

He started yelling at me saying all sorts of things. "Jane! I can handle this on my own. No one wants you to be smarty pants. Come on, you think that you are the top fighter and there is no one can be better than you, just because Bryan likes you!" Kevin said.

I was completely shaken at this moment, all I wanted to do was help Kevin out. The first time I met him, he seemed to be so nice. In anger I left him there and ran to catch up with the rest. Although I kept on thinking about what Kevin had said, and it bothered me everytime. Was I really like that and did Bryan... actually like me?

"Jane where are you?" interrupted my thoughts when I realized Anne was calling out for me. Following Anne's voice I found all of them. Anne on seeing me said "Goodness Jane don't disappear in a place like this".

I tried to completely forget and ignore what Kevin had said as I focused on what was in front of us. The Presage were building a massive. I took out my sword and then I heard a deep voice behind them say "*Terminer les tous! Attaque*".

The voice seemed to be familiar and in the next instant I realized it was Mal's voice. Wondering what that meant the next thing we did was attack. All of us with all our energy attacked the wall trying to get past it, yet the Presage didn't budge and instead I fell backward.

---

* *"Terminer les tous! Attaque"* = *Finish them all, attack*

Will then said "They are way too strong for us".

Anne then said "We need to use our inner power". So on the count of three two one thinking of my parents with all my energy I released the power within me. Bright light filled the area and the wall was gone, however something bigger waited for us behind them.

With the light gone something bigger emerged and I knew it was Mal.

I wasn't very surprised after all he had to show up what surprised me was that a Fonce of fire shot directly towards Mal and it came from behind. Although he easily deflected the Fonce I wondered who shot that. As I turned around I saw Kevin slightly bruised but still made it alive.

Mal then said "Of all the people him? honestly, you guys haven't got anyone better?"

With these words he lifted his hand along with which even Kevin rose as if there was a rope connecting both of them. Lifting Kevin up Mal pushed Kevin hard against the wall.

At that time I also noticed the peculiar madness in Kevin's eyes, the same madness, I had seen in him when he was yelling at me.

"Oh my god I know what happened to Kevin. He wanted to finish the quest alone. Which probably resulted in hatred, making things easy for Mal to manipulate Kevin" Lacey said. "Memories, think of times we all spent together" I blurted out thinking of what happened to Anne.

"Come on Kevin you are stronger than this, fight him. Remember how we got to Mr. Winsten, how we solved all the clues. All of us contributed" I said.

Although I was still mad I knew we needed him to finish this quest. Minutes passed as Lacey's silent tears rolled down her cheeks. I knew this had to work and Kevin would come back for all of us.

After a while Mal smirked, saying "Enough of your silly jokes. You might have defeated my spirits, but there's nothing beyond this".

There was a long pause, I wanted to finish him quickly, yet I could not, as without Kevin's power, our power was less.

Then he spoke "Somewhere deep within I was feeling really bad, for hurting people, destroying things and what Kevin was going through further added to this bad feeling... So I only ask for one thing and then I'll have peace".

At first, I was completely touched, but just as the next second passed I didn't believe a word he said. I am pretty sure it was all a trap.

Only Lacey didn't realize this and said "Agreed what do you want?".

"Anne, give me Anne," he said.

This time before Lacey tried to do anything I said "No way. Hell no. Anne is not going anywhere".

I turned and looked at Anne with wide eyes warning her from doing anything stupid.

Showing his anger to what I said, he shot a white Fonce. We dodged.

Will said to all of us "Anne this is just a trick don't get trapped. Also, guys Kevin is back. He is all right and guess what; the only thing he had to say was Lacey".

To what Will had just said Lacey blushed.

"We need to confuse him. Brain over brawn" Anne then said.

"Also, we need to get him angry so that he gets distracted" I added.

"Let's go," I heard someone say and then I saw Kevin running along with us.

We started to run all around the place in different directions.

"What the hell is going on!" Mal said.

"Only smart people can understand our moves definitely not you" I screamed as we all laughed continuing to run.

"Have you ever seen yourself in the mirror, do you realize how ugly you are," that one was said by Lacey.

"Nice one" Will commented.

I was having a lot of fun, way more than I expected to have. Mal was getting frustrated by the second and started to throw his Fonces in every direction possible, all of which missed us all by a wide margin.

"Your aiming skills are pathetic you should practice more in that" Kevin said.

"Or get glasses" Will added.

Both of them high fived and angrier than ever Mal started to throw Fonces even more aimlessly.

At this moment all of us now knew he didn't have any specific target now. This was it, there was no more running around, laughing or manipulating. So slowly we made a circle surrounding him, only he didn't realize it. On the count of three, two, one and thinking of my parents I released all the power within me. Our laughter echoed throughout the place but just when we thought the game was over for him he used his magic, in addition, started to attack us back. This hadn't happened last time. Last time only we attacked, he was caught off guard and we were good to go back to L'Abri with Ellie. Although we were five and he was a one man army he seemed to be stronger.

I put in all my energy and from the corner of my eye I saw that I wasn't the only one trying so hard. Anne, Lacey, Will and Kevin were trying just as hard.

I then heard Kevin scream "Everybody we just have to hold on for a little bit longer. We all know he is alone and that he has limited stamina. Once that stamina is over we can easily defeat him".

Kevin's idea did seem to make a lot of sense because no matter who you are, everyone has a limit. All of us kept a strong hold of our power while Mal continued to attack.

Although in the meantime we were forgetting that even we have limited stamina.

Lacey's voice then distracted me of my thoughts as I heard her say "I can't take this any longer".

"You have to hold on Lacey" Will screamed back.

Kevin then screamed "Guys he's losing energy every second. This is our last shot before we end up losing all our energy. This is it we have to go full blast now. And Lacey if I die I want you to know that I love you".

To that, I couldn't help but smile.

My hands were trembling and my legs couldn't bear the weight anymore. My breaths had become uneven and raged. But I couldn't give up yet just a few more seconds and I knew all of this pain would be over. So in case something happened to me I would want my parents and Bryan to know that I am very grateful for having them. Then taking in a deep breath I gave in all of the energy left within me. As if it were the last time I would ever do so.

A dim white light filled the area. Unlike last time it wasn't intense, just a soft glow. I saw Mal almost about to fall and then he said in muffled and hoarse voice "Love is a very powerful thing" after which he disappeared from our visions.

Was he gone or was he going to come back were questions that we didn't have an answer to. Although right now what we knew was that our job was over and it was time to get back. Without any further delay holding on to our pendant we said the portal rhyme

> *Portal of L'Abri*
> *We all are one or none*
> *Take us together*
> *Back up*

With the spinning feeling over, we got to the sea shore where I saw Mr. Winsten waiting for all of us. I couldn't stand any longer; I was about to give in and fall. I felt nauseous and the spinning feeling in my head just made things worse.

Before I knew it Mr. Winsten held my shoulder bringing me back to balance.

He held out a liquid inside a very small transparent capsule.

"This is called an *Aide*. It is given to Ultimates who need energy during the quest or after a major injury Not having much of choice I drank the liquid and my lightning bolt started to glow and then all of sudden most of pain and the fatigue I felt was gone. I smiled and thanked Mr. Winsten. Looking around I realized that I wasn't the only one who needed it. Will, Lacey, Anne and Kevin had some too.

Mr. Winsten then said "Aide is given during emergencies and fights. It is temporary and you'll feel the fatigue once again after a period of time. Also, this can harm us if not taken in proper dosage".

There was a pause but then Mr. Winsten continued "Anyways how was your quest? I thought of trying out another riddle, but then I realized you guys must be very tired," in a cheerful voice.

"Well, thank you, Mr. Winsten for your consideration," Will said. He sounded more relieved than thankful.

We drove towards L'Abri at a great speed. Holding on to our seats, we zoomed towards L'Abri ...

We stopped abruptly, so abruptly that we were nearly thrown off our seats.

Mr. Winsten then said "Now we are about to enter L'Abri so I request you guys close your eyes".

"But what if..." Kevin began.

Cutting Kevin short, Mr. Winsten said "If you don't close your eyes. Your eyes would be in danger if you don't close them. And trust me on this, unless you are planning to lose them".

I waited for all them to close their eyes. As I saw all of them close their eyes, including Kevin and not wanting to take any chance I closed mine too. I couldn't feel any change except that temperatures had risen. Not being able to bear the heat anymore I opened my eyes and realized that we reached L'Abri at last...

Chapter 12

Back with Victory

As soon as we reached I heard someone scream "Look they are all back!".

Soon a crowd had gathered in front of us. The crowd grew as people filled in althoughI didn't know or recognize any of them. Soon I could see Ellie, Cara and Abner but the one I wanted to meet wasn't in sight. I finally saw Bryan as he came out of the fighting arena covered in sweat. The crowd cheered and chanted for all of us. And the feeling was beyond words.

I turned to thank Mr. Winsten but he was long gone. The crowd silenced after a while and we went to our house. I was flat on the bed with every part of my body aching. Sleep didn't come so I just stared at the ceiling. I heard soft footsteps nearby, hoping it was Bryan's. I looked down and saw Bryan make his way up. Bryan for some reason seemed to be surprised to see me.

What happened?"

"You should be tired Jane I thought I would find you asleep" was his reply.

I went to kiss him, while Bryan said "I missed you".

I then began to tell him about the quest, but he stopped me saying "You ought to have rested".

While I waited to catch some sleep, I pictured our whole quest. On waking up I saw that it was dark outside and there wasn't a soul inside. I changed afterwhichI went directly towards the cafeteria assuming that's where everybody would be at this time.

Once I reached the cafeteria aroma of delicious food wafted through the air. I saw that everyone had already started to eat so I took my plate and food as well and sat next to Bryan.

Bryan saw me and said "We thought of waking you up but since you were sound asleep, we didn't want to disturb you".

After finishing dinner Ellie said she had to make an announcement. We all gathered in the auditorium whileI wondered what Ellie had to say. Once everybody assembled Ellie said "May I please call Kevin, Jane, Anne, Will and Lacey on stage. They shall tell us a wonderful story".

The five of us then made our way towards the stage. Just before we got on the stage I quickly asked Will, "What does

Ellie mean by a wonderful story?" sounding confused. Will laughed and said "Jane it obviously means our quest".

All of us took turns about telling all the other Ultimates about our quest. Will who didn't want to say much started first speaking about how we got out of L'Abri. Then I took the lead telling them about the crazy driver and our fight against the Presage. Anne then told everyone about Mr. Winsten's riddle and the noodles. While Lacey told them about how we go inside the underworld. Kevin concluded it with telling them about the fight. After we were done there was a round of applause as Ellie handed us all pearls, Anne and I received indigo. Both Will and Lacey got blue pearls while Kevin received a green pearl.

After the hooting and cheering was over all the Ultimates soon dispersed themselves. As we were about to go, Kevin, said "I need to tell you guys something"

"Sure" Lacey replied.

"When we were in the quest around near the portal I got this feeling that the quest was all mine. As crazy as it sounds it was like I had to do everything. I had to lead all of you and not work like a team. I had a feeling that I had to finish him single handedly, be superior then everybody after which something strange started to happen to me. I am really sorry guys and especially for screaming at you, Jane. I tried to fight it, when I got my senses back I could only hear you guys but couldn't reach you. Then all Will said was Lacey and I was back to normal, thanks Lacey for loving me and saving me" said Kevin.

Lacey looked at him and smiled, saying "I'm glad you are back".

I was still uncertain on forgiving Kevin but when I gave a thought from his perspective, I felt bad. Also, Kevin sounded so sincere, hence I forgave him.

I smiled and then said "Kevin as long as you never do that again".

"Never I promise" Kevin said.

"All of us forgive you" Anne said to which we all nodded. In that moment Kevin seemed to be the happiest person.

As we kept walking towards our houses we were stopped by Elie, Cara, Bryan and Abner who said we had to meet Sacre. I wondered why that was necessary as the quest was already over however then Will explained that we were going to meet Sacre to get insights on our quest and how we could have done better. As we reached the attic after climbing all of those stairs we called out for Sacre.

Sacre came out with the same tele mist and said "I must say that all of you did an extremely good job while the other one learned a lesson and to love".

Sacre continued saying "I am not the one to say what you should have done better because that is up to you to find your mistakes and reflect upon them. But I can tell you how Mal was defeated although I am not aware if fully or not. His blow was certainly stronger than any Ultimate could have taken but the fact that he had crumbled down was because none of you were ready to give up, all of you tried because you had something to live for, something to look forward to or something to change from the past. While Mal lived for the moment. He had nothing to live for or change. For him it was all just one world to conquer, one world to destroy and one war to win".

After saying these words Sacre went back inside the ruby moreover not having anything else to ask or say we went back to our houses. Despite the fact that I had slept a lot after the quest, sleep still came fast. Then I drifted, far far away where my dreams caught me...

I entered a room which I didn't recognize and saw someone was sleeping in a bed. I saw the face and immediately recognized it. It was Anne...

She seemed in trouble like as if she was going through a nightmare. It looked as if she was trying to fight something going in her head and then all of a sudden she screamed "Nooooo!" which caused a piercing pain in my head.

I woke up with my head buzzing. I wondered what Anne was trying to fight. Trying to stay calm I took some deep breaths telling myself that it was just a dream. Her voice echoed in my head causing my head to hurt. I went down with my head spinning. Trying hard to keep my balance I walked a little and then I sat on a bed. I didn't even know whose bed I sat on until I saw Bryan.

Bryan got up and looked at me completely baffled asking "Not getting sleep, huh?" "Yeah," I said

"Come here"

I reached out and hugged him. Although he was soon back to sleep I stayed awake unable to sleep, although feeling secure knowing that Bryan was there; close to me.

Things with Anne weren't good either. Her dreams started to trouble her. In her dreams, Anne saw herself wandering around L'Abri. She looked up and saw that it was getting dark. She heard the voices "jamais jamais mort mort" immediately knowing the Presage were here. Although that was nothing, the worst was yet to come, she then saw Mal. But she didn't see him in the underworld instead she saw him right above the L'Abri.

Anne was frightened and woke up screaming **"Nooooo!"**.

PART 3

CHAPTER 13

A NEW GAME

I woke up to see that it was almost time for dawn and that I was still in Bryan's bed. Then I saw Bryan come towards me knowing that I was awake, he kissed me on the forehead saying "I'll see you later".

I was expecting that he would wake me up and ask me to come to practice, but feeling really tired as well as sore I closed my eyes. I woke up as a stroke of sunlight hit my eyes with the clock saying 9:30. If I was in New York right now I would say I'm up early, but at L'Abri it means you have to get ready quickly or else you ain't getting breakfast.

I quickly changed and rushed to the cafeteria. There were hardly any Ultimates left when I reached. I finished breakfast having two sandwiches and milk after which I went to the fighting arena however to my disappointment I saw everyone coming out. As I went inside the fighting arena I saw Bryan sat there and I went to join him.

"You missed practice," he said

"Well..." I began not sure of what to say.

"You needed rest. We'll start off with some light cardio exercises an hour after lunch or so" he said blankly without any expressions.

"Sounds good to me," I said as we made our way towards the house.

Then there was an awkward silence till Bryan asked "Jane, are you feeling okay?"

"Yeah, why do you ask?" I asked bewildered.

"No just making sure by asking and" Bryan said hesitantly.

"And?" I asked becoming curious.

"Um, well yesterday night you came to my bed and..." He took a moment's time but continued.

"And you slept all fine until suddenly you squeezed my hand real tight saying Bryan please help me, please help her. You looked really worried and then I hugged you afterwards you relaxed and slept back".

I wondered how my face looked right now, hoping it wasn't as red as I thought it would be.

I wondered if I should tell Bryan about my dream but again it was just a dream. He looked at me as if he was waiting for an answer, although we still kept walking. We reached our house and I hadn't spoken a word yet. While Bryan went to his bunk I just followed him sitting down on his bed. He changed into a washed T-shirt and sat down next to me.

He softly whispered "Jane if you don't tell me who are you going to tell?".

I didn't even know what to say and just looked at him.

A smile found his face as he hugged me saying "Trust me".

Then I told Bryan about the dream and Anne. He listened quietly and after I was done all he said was "A meeting".

"Jane don't worry all of us are there to help one another" he added and walked away brightening everything around him. I got up and walked straight to the library in the university looking for Anne.

Once I entered the library I saw Anne sitting in one corner of the library. She sat there, with her glasses were perched on her nose while she was reading a huge book titled "Oneirology".

"Anne," I said softly, not wanting to disturb her. Anne was startled, turned around she closed the book and hastily put it away. I had a suspicious feeling. Anne never did anything like, this in fact. I wouldn't be surprised if I knew more about her than she did herself. This definitely meant that she was hiding something from me.

"I think you had a really bad nightmare yesterday".

Anne looked alarmed and her muscles tightened.

She then hesitantly said "Me? no, nothing happened, I slept wonderfully".

Smiling I said "Anne don't try to lie to me".

Anne then worried said "Jane, something is wrong, I know it is. All of us are in danger".

"We'll get through this," I said reassuringly.

Anne kept the book back as I waited for her outside the library hoping that she doesn't ask me what I feared.

"Jane, how did you know?" Anne asked.

"I know you inside out," I replied flatly

"Jane, be serious, how did you know?" Anne asked this time with slight fear.

"Relax Anne" I said and then told her about the dream I had.

After I was done, she said "I'm so sorry Jane, I didn't mean to put you through all this" feeling guilty.

"You think it's your fault, idiot?" I said.

"Jane, did you just call me an idiot?" Anne asked.

"Well, if your ears are functioning properly then yes!" I responded.

It was really funny how Anne hated being called an idiot and I always used it to annoy her.

Anne then almost shouting said, "I swear to...".

"To whom, smarty pants?" I replied back and started running.

Anne was so irritated now that she was literally shouting "Jane Frances Hastings get back here!".

I hesitated for a moment as it had a been long since anyone had addressed me by my full name but I nonchalantly replied "No way snail!" and began to sprint.

Well, to be honest I hadn't really expected her to run right back but seeing her I increased my speed. As we ran all around L'Abri it felt like we were small kids once again, who would run around the gardens. Finally, I stopped near a bench and Anne gave me a small scowl after which we burst out laughing.

We laughed so hard, even after all the quests and being away from mom and dad it felt really good bringing back those childhood days. After we finally managed to stop laughing, I wondered what Anne had seen in her dream, although I decided to keep that off for the moment. We walked towards the cafeteria to get some water and saw a few Ultimates making their way for lunch.

"That was fun!" Anne exclaimed cheerfully.

"It sure was" I replied back with a smile.

I had lunch, although I wasn't that hungry. After that I made my way towards my house, knowing that I have an hour or so to spend before Bryan called us for the practice. I didn't know what to do since I couldn't hang out with Anne as she had to work with other Malin Ultimates. I then suddenly realized that we were allowed to bring along one memory with us to L'Abri. I asked for my camera while Anne had asked for her diary. I kept all my memories in the camera my grandmom had gifted me when I was a small kid. I always kept that camera safe with me as it reminded me of my grand mom who had unfortunately passed away two years ago.

I went through pictures of my mom and dad, my birthdays along with all my friends at the amusement park. Pictures of Anne and I, our elementary school and then moving to high school. The memories seemed to run through my mind until it struck me that I don't have any pictures of Bryan or L'Abri. I was never a photographer but my friend Sean was, who in fact taught me how to click pictures. That's when Bryan came in and I clicked a picture of him. The flash took him by surprise and his face was priceless.

I started to laugh so much that I was now clutching onto to my stomach, which was sore from all the laughing.

"Hey!" Bryan said, slightly pouting, which made me laugh even harder.

He then took away my camera and started to see different pictures. As I stopped laughing and tried to breathe Bryan asked me "Those are your parents?".

I sat next to him and realized that he was seeing pictures of my basketball matches.

"Yup, I miss them so much" I replied back.

"Oh" was all he said, but there was something sad about the way he said it maybe something much more than just oh.

Changing the topic, I asked "Bryan do you play basketball?".

"Yup, I played basketball as well and made it to the Varsity team but my game was football. What about you?".

"I play basketball, I love that sport and miss it just as much as I miss my parents" I replied with a sigh.

"What about Anne?" he then asked.

"She was a Badminton player. She had it within herself and wanted to be a player along with studies while I always wanted to get into WNBA".

"Cool, but now let's go to practice" Bryan said getting up.

We reached the fighting arena and warmed up within the arena. We kept running for a while without saying a word and then did different exercises starting from the head, forearms, then going to the core and finishing with the legs. As soon as we finished the last exercise I collapsed on the bench. And Bryan joined soon.

"Well, I thought you explicitly said that we would be doing light cardio" I said to which Bryan only smiled.

As we headed back to our houses covered in sweat. "Bryan can I ask you something?". "Yeah sure" he replied.

"What do all the other Ultimates do at L'Abri?. I mean do they ever get to go back to their old lives?".

"Jane you must understand that we are created to keep the Niasis safe. You may call the Niasis humans or the ordinary man. We want peace in the world and make it a better place in the future. We were the chosen ones by them".

Bryan then stopped, and looked at my confused face as I wondered who were them?.

He continued saying "Them could be anyone. It could be the angels or the gods or the protector of the universe. We all believe that who ever they might be, they want peace as well. Now answering your question the Ultimates come to learn here. If you are a Soins then you learn to mainly cure

people and find cures. Soins were the people who made the
Aide. But that doesn't mean they only do that. They learn
how to fight and study at the university about history of
our L'Abri, methods to fight, logical reasoning and values
of life. L'Abri is our home however at the same time L'Abri
is also somewhat like a school. Now since you belong to
Audacieux you spent most of your time in the fighting arena
but as you become better we'll also teach you how to cure
and various other Malin skills. Now after you have finished
your training, in the end it's your choice. Everything is your
choice. It's your choice whether to stay or leave. If you want
to leave and get back to your old life then you are given a
forgetting liquid. Once you drink that your memory of this
place will be washed away and so will your ability to use
magical powers. Or you could leave and but still be in touch
with L'Abri. You could work as an agent or help us with the
weapon making unit etc. But once you become an Ultimate
even if you decide to leave, you still remain an Ultimate.
Although your lightning bolt fades away we can always still
call you in times of war".

Bryan took a deep breath and then said "Wow that was a lot
talking and explaining".

I just smiled and replied "A lot to take in as well".

We reached our house and I went to have a shower. As I took
a shower I just kept thinking about all this. Why were we
the chosen ones?. Why is Sacre still here looking out for all
of us?. If he had, to then why in that small attic and closed
in a box?. There were so many things yet to know.

After I changed Bryan came to my bunk. I tried to brush my questions away but before I could Bryan said "Looks like you have lots to ask".

I just looked and Bryan said "I just keep wondering why us of all people?. Why is Sacre always in the attic?. Why do we fight Mal? And so many other questions...".

"Hmm. That's not unusual. Jane, you are an Ultimate and you have every right to know. But I must say you are very curious and you obviously aren't tired of listening to my voice".

I just smiled and Bryan started to speak. "Jane we were chosen because we aren't ordinary. Because we have something to offer to this world and there are very few of us. I don't know what they saw in us but this is the truth, we are meant to do much more. I can't tell you why Sacre is in the attic yet. I'll surely tell you one day but when it's the right time. And we fight Mal because he wants to harm the Niasis and rule over them. In the end, all he wants is full control and power over the world. But before he does that he has to finish us and our kind. You have been to two quests Jane tell me what were common in both quests?".

"Well, we fortunately won both the quests and I got tired in both the quests?" I replied not sure if I was right.

Bryan then continued "Jane that's true but you must have noticed that he has no human warriors along with him. Only the Presage. Mal is almost close to becoming a robot.

It's his illness which is driving him mad. He lacks emotion. He doesn't love, have hope or faith, doesn't believe, doesn't care the only thing he can feel is anger and hatred. He assumes that conquering the world will help him. But in the same time, he also knows that a possible cure which will make him much stronger is at L'Abri. I don't know what is the cure, where it is or even if something like that exists. But if it does exist then we have protect it. Whatever it maybe. And the only person who knows about it is Sacre. We have tried to ask him what it is but he always says "Sometimes knowing too much can be dangerous. Sometimes it's just better to leave some mysteries unsolved. Better for us and the rest..."

I just quietly listened to what Bryan said and I did make a lot of sense out of it.

I then smiled and said "Thank you Bryan for letting me know".

"Anytime" he said but then immediately looking excited he said "I can't wait for tonight". "Why?" I asked curiously.

"Well, you'll get to know in a few hours" he replied looking outside the window.

"Please!" I said, trying to sound as nice as I could and seeing that he said "Ooh we'll have so much fun".

"Pretty please," I asked once again

"I got a feeling that tonight's gonna be a good night," he sang and walked out.

I let out a groan and he turned saying "I'm stubborn!" giving away a smile which was evil but at the same time adorable.

I lay on my bunk wondering what to do when I saw lots of people make their way outside the door. Not having anything to do anyway, I decided to follow them.

Only knowing Kevin among the crowd I asked him "Where are we going?".

"To practice," he said in a very casual way.

"Where?" I asked, baffled.

"At the university" he replied back.

"Huh?" I asked still confused.

"Jane, I think you haven't done this before. So we'll be given some situations and we'll have to solve them. It's like we are in our own quest. It's a monthly exercise. They are usually easy, so don't worry" Kevin replied reassuringly.

"Oh, thanks Kevin,"

"No problem".

As we entered the university nervousness and excitement ran throughout me. Instead of taking the elevator all of us decided to sprint through the stairs. We finally stopped at the fifth floor if I was counting right. We stopped in front of the door and a lady handed us a purplish liquid in a test tube. I thought twice before I touched that liquid to my lips. I looked around to see everyone drank it without any hesitation. As I let the liquid go down my throat. I realized that it didn't taste all that bad after all. It was sour at the beginning, but as it went down it tasted sweeter.

I blinked and all of a sudden it felt like everything was spinning around real fast, althoughI stood in the center, still. Then from the corner of my eye I saw two white, Fonces coming towards me. They looked exactly like how Mal's white, Fonces looked like. I immediately bent as both the Fonces passed just above my head. Standing up I became more alert and watched around me.

Then I saw another Fonce come towards me, I bent away, however the Fonce bent along with me. I knew this time bending wouldn't help me so I released a Fire Fonce from my hands making Mal's white Fonce disintegrate. There was a moment of silence after which Mal's white Fonces started to come from all directions. They came towards me at high speed and my body started to tense up not knowing what to do. I could shoot down one of Mal's Fonce. Although I couldn't run the risk of getting wounded by the ones that I couldn't shoot. As I braced myself to take hits from those Fonces., I thought of my mom and dad saying "Please protect me", I squeezed my eyes tightly shut, knowing that I'll get hurt.

After a while when I opened my eyes I saw that the Mal's White, Fonces were gone, in addition I also saw that there was a shield around me. I took a step forward and the shield was gone as I heard a lady robot voice saying "Congratulations Jane you've successfully completed level 1".

Purple mist covered everything in a jiffy and after a few seconds it also cleared on its own, then I saw a door which read exit. I walked down the stairs to see that not many of the Ultimates had finished yet and that it was already dark.

I went to the house, changed afterward went to the cafeteria. By the time I reached most of the people had arrived. I wondered what Bryan was talking about when Ellie had interrupted my thoughts.

"Ultimates attention, please, today we'll have our traditional game after three months. This time the dividing house is Soins and as soon as the clock ticks 9:00 we shall begin".

We hooted, screamed and cheered as we began our dinner. Though I had no clue what their traditional game was, but I was still excited to be a part of it. We had a hearty dinner with half an hour still left.

After a while, Abner said "As you all know we'll be playing our usual Ultimate capture the flag.,".

Oh capture the flag were games which I read in books, but playing it in real life was going to be totally cool.

Abner then explained the rules "Not only are you supposed to keep your opponent's flag safe, in addition you also have to get your flag back from them. Once you have your flag as well as your opponent's flag with you, keep them next to each other and you've won the game. If by chance the teams have one another's flag, then we restart".

There were twenty minutes left for 9:00 as the Soins team started to split up. I knew Anne wouldn't be in our team since she was in Malin but I still kept my fingers crossed hoping that Lacey would be on our team. The teams were made and unfortunately Lacey wasn't in our team, which left me with Kevin and Bryan. We had another ten minutes left and both the teams went in the opposite direction. Then some Ultimates handed us strange looking guns.

I wondered if the guns had actual bullets when Bryan said "Everybody please pay attention! This works like any other ordinary gun, but instead of releasing a bullet it releases a laser which temporarily paralysis your body".

All of us then formed a circle to discuss our strategy, such as where to hide our flag, who would do what etc.

"Kevin and you take charge of defense" Bryan said, pointing to a guy I didn't recognize

"But..." Kevin began,

"I want to go for offense" Kevin said

"Kevin you are strong in defense" Bryan said flatly.

"Jane and Rick could go for defense" Kevin said pointing to the same guy.

Just as I was about to say I don't mind as if reading my mind Bryan said "Jane, I'm keeping you close to me, moreover you are an offensive player and Kevin can handle defense well." Although in a whisper making sure only I could hear him.

Trying to change the topic, I asked "Where should we keep the flag?".

"I was wondering how about under the soil?" a girl from Soins suggested.

"Brilliant idea" someone commented and all of us agreed.

Then a small boy who was about fourteen suggested "How about hiding the flag here and then defending somewhere else, that way they will be confused and will end up searching the wrong place".

"What an idea!, transported from Malin?" Bryan asked the kid.

The kid then gleefully said "Born with Audacieux till the last breath with Audacieux".

Impressed by his answer I started to clap and soon everyone else joined. While the big grin on his face was priceless.

"Although we should still keep at least a few people for defense here just in case" someone else commented.

"Yeah, we'll do that," I heard someone else say.

I hardly recognized the Ultimates atL'Abri, so I usually smiled at whoever I saw. Then all of us started to hide the flag after which we got ourselves prepared for defense, While the rest of us were for offense.

As we waited for Ellie to give the signal I wondered where they could have kept our flag. L'Abri is pretty big further more they could have hidden the flag anywhere absolutely anywhere. I looked up to see the stars shining along with which I saw the University's tower, the highest point at L'Abri. Bryan then came towards us informing us that even the other team was ready and all that was left was Ellie's signal. We finally heard Ellie say "Let the games begin!". Hearing this commotion broke out.

All of us stayed close together at the beginning, but the Malin defense was way too strong and tight everywhere. So then we split up in twos and threes. All of us split and silently walked making sure that no one saw us.

We continued walking when all of a sudden Bryan pulled me down "Ouch! I exclaimed seeing a laser go just above me while Bryan shot someone from Soins.

Both of us then began to sprint while Bryan shot lasers all around the place almost making it look like one of those disco nights. We then stopped and I saw that we were near the University. I looked up as I had an idea as to where the Malin could have hidden our flag. I wasn't really sure, but my instincts told me that the flag should be up there. I quickly whispered to Bryan that I had a feeling that our flag was on top of the university.

He took a minute then in hushed whispers replied "Jane that's not possible our flag and all the other house flags are always there at the university top.

"Bryan they are Malin they probably hid it there to mislead us. I am going up and checking it out" I replied.

Right then I spotted a boy from Malin hiding behind the pillar and shot him. He immediately collapsed to the ground. I then ran faster than I usually would with Bryan right beside me.

Bryan didn't say much at first but then when he made sense out of what I had said, he replied "Oh my god Jane your a..." Bryan said while shooting a girl behind us "genius" he completed.

"Okay, so you go and get the flag and I'll watch out" he said

"No way I'm not leaving you behind". I replied back not giving him an option.

"Uh" he groaned "Who knew my girlfriend was so ?"

At the word girlfriend, shivers ran down my spine tensing my body up. But I quickly let that thought go of me as we entered the University.

I was going to take the stairs when Bryan pointed the elevator. As soon as we entered the elevator we shot two Malin boys before they could even spot us. We reached the last floor and not seeing anyone we got out. Thanks to my observation and Bryan's quick reflex we shot a girl from Malin, who was about to pull the trigger. We took the stairs which would lead us to the terrace. We immediately spotted two happy Soins girls, busy chatting and shot them before they could finish their gossip. We reached the terrace and I spotted our red flag.

Then without warning something from behind hit me and the pain was immense. I immediately fell to the ground after which I heard a laser release and Bryan screaming "Jane!". It felt like all my bones were broken at once while a piercing pain shot through my spine. Before I could say anything else darkness spread before my eyes. When I woke up, I saw blurred images of Bryan shaking me vigorously and screaming my name. After a split second I suddenly got up and started laughing without any pain at all.

"God Bryan, I have never seen you so scared" I said.

"Scared because I care, idiot" he replied back, squeezing me in a bear size hug.

I got up and ran towards the flag, carefully taking it out.

Bryan then said "Even Malin can make careless mistakes sometimes" handing me the original Audacieux flag which was kept on the side. I quickly replaced it so it wouldn't make a difference. We went down quickly making sure that we weren't seen. We ran as fast as our legs could take us to the place where we hid their flag. Going back seemed to be easier than entering. We quickly reached, dug out their flag which was still safe.

Bryan then said "Overlap both the flags".

"No, we overlap both the flags" I said

"Nope to your idea and I listened to you there, you listen to me now" Bryan replied back.

I rolled my eyes and overlapped both the flags.

As soon as both the flags touched each other the combined light from both flags lit up the place and fireworks exploded.

"Jane has got the flag, Audacieux wins!!" I heard Ellie scream.

A crowd of Ultimates gathered around us cheering. I saw Anne, who seemed to be happier than me. God knows what

I would have done without my best friend. Although more than half the credit obviously went to Bryan, I still felt happy believing in my instincts and getting the flag.

With everyone having enjoyed the game and completely exhausted, we made our way towards our house.

Chapter 14

Something that has never happened before

Bryan left me on my bunk kissing me good night and before I could even change from my sweaty clothes, I was fast asleep. A few hours later I started to feel that something was just not right. I woke up and saw that it was still dark outside. I went outside to see fog all around, quite unusual for this time of the year. I then saw some more Ultimates come out and Bryan was up right next to me. Everyone else also seemed to be just as confused as I seemed to be. I spotted Ellie, who was looking terrified. I turned to ask Bryan for an explanation and he seemed to know exactly what was going on. But just like Ellie even he was terrified.

Bryan looked at me and then said "Jane this isn't fog this is mist. Not just ordinary mist, but…."

"Then?" I asked

"It's Sacre," he completed.

"What? But Sacre has only come out when he's called out," I said with lots of other questions running in my mind.

Bryan didn't say another word but just froze at what he saw. I didn't know what else to do except watch. Most of the L'Abri was awake by now. I found Anne in the crowd of Malin to see she was baffled herself. The mist, then began to speak just like how Sacre did.

"The destroyer of L'Abri could be the saviour of L'Abri or saviour could be the destroyer of L'Abri. Now it's the Ultimate's choice to make the ultimate decision".

Then, instead of going back into the box in the attic, it turned bright white, vanished just as quickly as it came. Silence swept the whole of L'Abri as all of us were too shocked to speak.

While all of us wondered who Sacre was talking about when Ellie spoke "Ultimates, what you all just saw has never happened in the past, Sacre came out of the attic on his own and now is gone, this only goes to show us that danger is coming closer. None of us here know who the rogue Ultimate is and you never know it could be you, it could be me, it could be anybody. Please keep your eyes and ears open and try to protect one and another and take care of L'Abri. We are all tired now so we all ought to take some rest. Please disperse to your respective houses".

Terror was all around the home. Was L'Abri no more, a safe place to stay?. Dispersal was quiet and no one dared to utter a word. I reached my bunk with Bryan and as he was about to go, I asked him "What will we do now without Sacre? And what..."

Bryan cut me short saying "Shh get some sleep and as of now no one has an answer". Although right now, I had thousands of questions. Unwillingly, I closed my eyes.

I woke up realizing that it's well past dawn. Although I still saw more than half the Ultimates still asleep, I changed and went to the fighting arena. As I reached I saw Bryan and a few other Ultimates.

On seeing me Bryan said "Join".

They were practicing both offensive and defensive slides. After five more repetitions along with more Ultimates joining in, we started our fitness routines. We started with some jogging then on to some supposedly light on the spot run and finally finishing with sprinting. It was time for breakfast.

As we were all about to make our way towards the cafeteria Bryan stopped us and said "I want everyone back after lunch but you are free after breakfast till lunch".

All of us were done with our breakfast faster than we usually do with an awkward silence throughout L'Abri.

After breakfast, I noticed Anne and I asked her, "Should we tell Ellie about our dreams, although Bryan said he would ask for a meeting".

To that, Anne replied "We'll anyway have to tell her one day or other moreover the faster the better it'll be".

So both of us made our way towards Ellie's office, hoping she'll not be too busy. When we opened the door to our surprise, we saw Abner, Bryan and Cara all of them there. Seeing that they were all in an intense conversation, Anne and I apologized and went to wait outside.

As we were about to go out when Ellie in her usual friendly tone said "Join us and sorry? for what?".

To that Anne and I couldn't help but smile.

I started off "We came here to tell all of you something which might mean trouble". I then continued by telling them about my dream.

. After I was done there was a pause as everyone waited for Anne to say something. Knowing how secretive Anne was, I knew she wouldn't feel comfortable in front of so many people, still she started hesitantly.

"I saw L'Abri burned down, many Ultimates dead and he was inside the home. He said, *"Come with me or this will be the future of L'Abri very soon."* Anne almost choked on the last words.

"We need to be strong and be always be on guard," Ellie said.

"Bryan, start guarding from today," she continued

"On it" was Bryan's reply.

Cara then said "I'll get all the supplies ready in case anything goes wrong".

"Good and Abner double check all the security to make them tighter" Ellie said to hear

"Got it"

With nothing more to say all of us left the office. Bryan and I walked towards our house while I wondered what to do.

Bryan then asked "Got anything to do?"

"Nope" I replied, shaking my head.

"Okay then let's go for some analytical thinking and game strategies" Bryan said.

He turned to look at me and I gave the blankest expression I ever have because I didn't get a word he said. He stared at me for a few seconds and then completely cracked up. He was almost on the ground half laughing and half mumbling words saying

"Jane, that clueless face of yours, Oh my god!" now gasping for some air.

"What?" I asked more confused.

Finally, almost done with laughing he said "God Jane you are so dumb".

"No, I'm not!" I yelled back sticking my tongue out. I started to walk the other way in a huff, hearing some footsteps behind obviously being Bryan's.

He whispered in my ears, "You are dumb".

I thought he had come to apologize, what an idiot. He then ran the other way. He was jogging and this time I needed to get him.

I ran close behind him and just as I was really close Bryan said "Holy!" definitely not expecting me to catch up with him and started running faster.

Just as we were nearing the cafeteria, without him noticing me, I planned to go around the cafeteria while he would keep running straight then I would stop right in front of him. As I kept running I was taken aback by surprise when I saw Bryan right in front of me.

"Think I didn't see you?" he said with a slight smirk on his face.

I didn't know what to say and that's when Bryan kissed me.

"God Jane you are brave and someone whom you can have fun with also at the same time you are most trustworthy and almost the smartest person that I have ever met" he said.

For that, I smacked him in his arm playfully.

"Ouch! What was that for? I was only complementing you", Bryan said.

"That was for only saying, almost," I replied back.

To that I saw something behind those playful eyes, something sad. Anyway, I managed to smile from ear to ear and how much ever Bryan teased, chased, scolded, drained me I still loved him no matter what. We walked towards our house yet I was still confused.

I asked "Bryan you know what, I still didn't get what you were trying to say" to that he just looked at me and shook his head.

We reached our house and I was still waiting for an answer.

Then Bryan said "Everybody line up".

Soon enough a group of curious Audacieux Ultimates lined up as Bryan said "All of us are now going to the University. It's more or less like your usual monthly tests except here you only need more of your head" pointing at his head almost pouting.

Oh God! The L'Abri was turning out to be like school with so many tests.

We reached the University and were handed the same purple potion that we were given before. As soon as I swallowed the potion I felt everything around me spin, then as everything around me started to slow down I saw Bryan to my left and both my parents to my right. On seeing my parents a warm sensation flowed through me comforting me. The thought of me being away from them for so long saddened me, although my thoughts were then interrupted by a voice. A voice I have heard often enough to recognize. It was Mal's voice.

He said, "They stand on your either sides, choose one of them Jane, be wise".

I looked at both sides, Bryan on one side and family on the other. How to choose was the only thing that ran through my head. Obviously family, but I couldn't leave Bryan. He was like an angel to me always helping me out taking care of me. I also knew that if Bryan was here, then he would definitely not leave me.

I was still in a state of confusion, when I heard Mal say "I don't have all day, choose or else both of them shall be destroyed. One, two, three...".

That's when a brilliant idea struck me. I rushed towards Bryan and grabbed his hand. As soon as I touched him, he came to life and stood there smiling at me. The next second I saw a white, Fonce going towards my parents. With all my force I tried to block the Fonce, but I didn't have enough power. Suddenly the white, Fonce disintegrated, when Bryan puts in all his power too. I knew Bryan would help me and save my parents. My parents then began to walk towards me and I squeezed them both in a hug, then my dad asked Bryan to join in who only silently watched us. This was one of the best feelings I had in a long time. Both my parents were close to me and so was Bryan.

Everything suddenly went away when I heard the lady's voice say "You have successfully completed this level". Things started to revolve fast yet again although this time I felt slightly claustrophobic. I then noticed that I was trapped inside a transparent box, in front of me, I saw a place very recognizable soon realizing that it was L'Abri but being destroyed. It was exactly like how Anne had described in her dream. Then getting a clear view I saw Bryan surrender... what the hell is going?. In times like this Bryan had to fight, he is the best fighter. I was confused and angry at the same time. I watched more of L'Abri getting destroyed, more of Ultimates getting injured or losing their lives. I couldn't stand this anymore. Then I saw the face of the person who was destroying everything, the person I wanted to fight and kill right now. I was taken aback by shock when I realized that the destroyer was someone I saw every morning, in front of the mirror.

No, I couldn't be doing this. Was Sacre talking about me?. Was this showing the future of L'Abri ?. Was I going to destroy everything? I thought.

"Get me out of here!", I screamed as I started to hit the glass furiously it could not be me. I know it just couldn't be me. I hit the glass once more, but to my disappointment not even the faintest crack appeared on the glass. I started to scream wanting the other me to hear me, telling her to stop. It seemed as if the whole world had all of a sudden turned deaf. That's when I knew nothing would work so I just closed my eyes and tried to forget whatever I just saw, my instincts told me that I wouldn't do anything like this. I would never hurt the people I love. I took a deep breath and when I opened my eyes, I saw L'Abri, the usual peaceful L'Abri. I smiled, knowing that the destroyer was never even me.

Now the glass box had disappeared and I heard the robot lady's voice, "You have completed this level successfully".

My surroundings started to swirl around once again at such high speed that my head started aching. As things started to slow down I realized that I was placed on top of a circular platform in the center of a room. I saw two things form in front of me as well as behind. I waited for a clear view and heard the lady robot voice again.

She said "This level Jane is not tiring, all you need to do is either take a step forward or take a step backward" and her voice trailed off.

Now in front of me, I could see two symbols which I would have seen too many times, to not recognize. While behind me, I could see L'Abri how I saw it when I first came along with Anne, Bryan and my parents and my friends back in New York. In front of me, towards the right, I saw my dream University, Harvard and to the left was my love of life WNBA. Normal girls of my age desire a perfect prom date, hot guys, makeup, etc. While I desired only these two things.

Turning back I saw my parents, my friends, L'Abri, Anne and Bryan. If I took a step back then it meant that I would leave the things I have always wanted at the same time if I took a step forward I would leave the people who have meant the world to me. I was utterly confused when suddenly something struck me.

I remember my mom used to always say "Lots of people and things come and go, but some people always stay with you all through, even through hard times".

"Why would they stay mama?" I would ask my mom.

Her reply would always be, "Because, they had enough faith in you and although you couldn't achieve whatever you wanted now you would achieve it sooner or laterwith their help and support".

Immediately I took a step back, although I had a slight desire to still get what I've always wanted. With that the lady robot voice said "Congratulations Jane your evaluations are over". With that the swirling stopped and I made my way towards the exit. I headed out the door and went to our house. All the thinking had really drained me out. I reached the house andsaw Bryan along with a few other Audacieux Ultimates, all of them were sitting in a circle. Then one girl amongst them looked up and said "Hi Jane".

I didn't know her, but I smiled and said "Hey".

I saw that they were all playing UNO when one guy gave me some cards and asked me to join

I thanked him and found that I was soon laughing hard with all of them. It had been quite a while since I had played UNO. There was a guy with golden blonde hair whose name was Austin, who had a good sense of humor.

"Jane" he asked and

"Yeah," I replied back throwing a blue 7 card.

"Is your mom a painter?".

"No," I said and wondered what a ridiculous question that was.

"Why would you ask".

"Well, she created a Masterpiece" he replied back.

I chuckled at him, saying "Thank you".

At my puzzled expression everybody laughed. Finally as laughing had stopped, Austin yelled "UNO!" I knew what that meant. He had only one card left and was going to finish the game soon.

"Yeah, right, I can see four other cards under your leg" a guy next him said. "Damn you! Alex" Austin replied back recognizing Alex was the one who gave me the cards. The game was soon ended with a girl on the other end throwing her last card. After the game, all of us made our way towards the cafeteria, knowing that it is time for lunch.

As we walked towards the cafeteria Bryan said "You guys get two hours of break after lunch. But then we have some hardcore practice to do".

"Okay" we all said in unison.

CHAPTER 15

NOW THAT'S WHAT I CALL FUN!

As we started to have our food Bryan teased me saying "Jane now did you get what analytical thinking meant?" to which I just rolled my eyes playfully.

"Anyway, how was it?" Bryan asked.

In reply, I moved my fingers around my chin pretending to be thinking hard. "It was pretty cool actually".

"Wow Jane so much thinking for that" Bryan chuckled.

I had a slight temptation to tell him about the situation and wondered what he would have done. But the food was just too overwhelming. After lunch, I met Anne, who came towards me. Her face was lit up so bright that I knew she had some good news.

She saw me and exclaimed "Jane! Oh my god today we tried this really cool stuff, but first you need to know this. Did you know that the border of the L'Abri was protected by love?. The warmth of all the Ultimates at L'Abri protects us, so indirectly we all protect one another. But unfortunately, even if one Ultimate doesn't contribute or is frightened in any way the boundary is supposed to possess a flaw".

Anne stopped to catch a breath and again continued, "So today we. All of us created an extra protective wall on top of the wall of love just in case that wall breaks or poses a flaw". "Good job genius," I told Anne, who was smiling from ear to ear.

"Thanks Jane" she the replied.

Then I said "Don't you think it's so cool that we always have our breaks together?". To that Anne face palmed herself. Wow now that wasn't something I was expecting.

"God Jane it surprises me how sometimes my best friend gets so candid" Anne then said.

"Shut up smarty pants," I told Anne simultaneously punching her in the arm.

"Ouch," she complained but explained "See Jane the reason why we have ours breaks together is because, Bryan, Abner, Cara and Ellie have their meeting, which gives us some time".

"Oh", I said, feeling dumbfounded.

"How do you know Anne? Bryan never said anything like that," I asked Anne.

"It's kind of obvious Jane, and even Abner didn't say anything" Anne replied back.

"Anyways, we are about to do something really cool" Anne said finally changing the topic.

"Oh, what is it?" I asked, letting curiosity get the best of me.

"Hold it my friend, it's something that Will told me.." Anne said her cheeks turning crimson red. "Ooh" I said and eyeing her.

"Shut up Jane just go get some clothes and call Kevin" Anne said, knowing exactly what I meant.

"Okie dokie" I replied back with a smile on my face and running away singing "love is in the air".

And without doubt I heard Anne yell back "I swear to god Jane!".

I ran away and quickly reached our house. I spotted Kevin near the corner lifting weights. Wow, I should take some inspiration. On seeing me Kevin quickly put the weights away and asked "Jane what brings you here?". "Well get a towel we are going to do something really cool" I replied back knowing exactly what the next question was going to be.

"Where are you taking me?". After which he said, see if it's a date you know I... Before he could even complete his sentence I impatiently said "Don't ask me apparently Will has planned something really cool for us. And moreover I have better things to do than ask you on a date".

I got my clothes ready. He came out holding a towel and I came out with my spare clothes and we headed towards the cafeteria.

"Lacey will be there too" I informed Kevin, who looked at me and said "Why are you jealous Jane?".

"Nope, absolutely not" I replied back with disgust god, I can never understand guys.

We continued to walk in silence until I spotted Anne, Lacey and Will at the cafeteria.

"Okay, that's everybody" Will said, sounding satisfied.

"I don't know why I am here Will and if it isn't worth it, I will murder you because I was doing important work" Kevin said.

"Oh look at Mr. Workaholic everybody" Will sniggered and we couldn't help but laugh.

"Don't worry Kevin I assure you, it's much better than whatever you were doing" Will continued his retort.

Will started to move and all of us followed him silently, getting more curious with every second. We soon reached the forest and saw the tree nymphs and the elves on the way. As we went deeper inside, Anne waved at them who happily waved back. We went deeper and deeper crossing the dense forest and finally reached a beautiful scenery. Will didn't stop and we kept walking. It felt like with each step we took we were going higher.

That's when Lacey sighed "I'm tired, how much more walking Will?"

"Almost there Lacey" Will replied back.

It felt like a year had already passed when Will finally stopped and said "We are here everybody".

We had climbed up to a good height and under us there was a crystal clear lake and we were covered by forest by all the sides and at a far stretch we could see L'Abri too. After finishing admiring the view I saw Will and Kevin take off their shirts and that's when I realized that we were going cliff diving.

Looking at my reaction Will said "That's right guys we are going cliff diving".

Will and Kevin jumped down and hit the water.

"Oh my god!!" I exclaimed. Although I never really feared the height this one was a bit too much and I looked down just to see if Kevin and Will were still alive. I looked at Anne and she winked, on her cue I counted 3,2,1 and both of us then jumped. Anne and I then hit the water together, water and as soon as we surfaced we screamed "That was awesome!".

Anne and I ran back up definitely ready for another dip. We reached up to see only Lacey wasn't wet yet.

"Guys, I'm afraid of heights" she exclaimed nervously. That's when without Lacey noticing Kevin crept behind her and pushed Lacey. Taken by surprise all we heard was Lacey scream. Kevin jumped right after her and soon a huge splash was created. We cheered for both of them.

After which we heard Lacey scream "Oh my god!" while Kevin smiled innocently showing his white pearly teeth. I saw both of both of them come out of the water, then I saw Kevin started to run while Lacey started to chase.

I said "Ooh, looks like someone's in trouble". Will and Anne then came along to see, Kevin finally stopped and sat down.

Lacey sat next to him and was literally screaming "Kevin how could..."

Kevin then shushed Lacey placing his finger on her lips "Admit it you had fun. I know you did". Lacey looked at him for a second and then kissed him. Kevin froze for a minute, obviously taken aback by surprise and this being their first kiss. But then Kevin kissed back. While they continued to kiss not knowing if I should look or not I looked at Anne who was already looking at me. We made an eye contact while Anne mouthed the word "awkward". While I agreed with her, a part of me also felt happy for them.

Lacey then stood and said "Let's do it again" having the widest grin on her face. All of us laughed and decided to go together on the count of three, two and one. All of us screamed and the splash was immense. For a moment I thought all the water from the lake was in the air.

Suddenly I realized that Bryan had called for practice and it had been a while since we were here. I looked at Kevin and he immediately nodded, saying "Guys, we gotta go, Bryan's called for practice and honestly I want to be able to breathe tomorrow".

At that, all of us laughed. I quickly changed into my spare clothes in the cover of the huge trees in the forest.

I heard Anne say "We should do this more often" to which Kevin said "True that".

Not wanting to be late Kevin and I ran as quickly as we could towards the fighting arena. We reached the fighting arena trying to catch our breath. "Phew" I let out a long breath, that was a hell of a run.

We entered the fighting arena to see everyone intently listening to what Bryan had to say. Bryan looked at Kevin and me, almost glaring at us, but calmingly saying "Please be seated". "Yeah, trust me, that was just the beginning. Bryan can get worse, he is a silent killer" Kevin said as we found a bench behind the rest of the Ultimates.

Bryan then said "Today we'll learn to control our power and on how to do it. This power is controlled not by your physical power, but by your mental power. So here you need a strong mind not just a strong body. We first think of the things or people that we love the most then focus on letting the power slowly through our hands in the right amount at the precise spot. This can be a little hard no doubt, but nothing is impossible. Let's get this started!"

We cheered and took our positions. So I thought of my parents who were beaming at me. I then tried to focus on my power, but it felt like something slipped away and boom a Fonce out of my hands.

On seeing the Fonce zoom towards people, Bryan deflected it safely before it could hurt anyone.

He admonished me teasingly "Watch it Jane you aren't planning to kill somebody now or are you?

Despite the fact that I didn't say anything, I was definitely embarrassed. But then determination was replaced and I knew I had to get it right this time by hook or by crook. I took it slowly this time, taking in a deep breath and letting it out slowly. I again thought of my parents who still stood there beaming at me and on getting my power I shut my eyes tight. I focused really hard, maybe the hardest I ever have and then slowly released the Fonce. I opened my eyes to see it was exactly like how I wanted it to be. Bryan immediately spotted the change and looked impressed.

"Got hang of it so soon?" he said with a questioning look.

"Looks like I wasn't planning to kill anyone after all" I said and Bryan smiled at my comment.

I did try a few more times but got exhausted afterward. Bryan let us have a break while we waited for some Ultimates who were yet to finish their practice and made our way towards the cafeteria for dinner. As we walked towards the cafeteria, I wondered how time just flew by. While we were having our dinner Ellie made an announcement. All I heard her say was something about Audacieux guarding L'Abri, but I zoned out way too busy with my food. After our dinner, we reached our house and Bryan then appointed some people to guard certain parts of the L'Abri.

"Kevin you take some people along with you and guard Ellie's office".

"Got it" Kevin replied back.

"But I don't think taking Jane with me is an option, is it? Guess she'll probably be with you".

Bryan smirked to that "I'm afraid my friend, but that's true,".

Wow, possessive much?. Bryan continued appointing more people, but I didn't bother to pay attention, knowing that I'll be with Bryan. When everyone took their positions, it left only Bryan and me in the room. There was a moment of silence and before it could get awkward I asked "What do we do now?".

Bryan puts on a mischievous smile, letting me know something was definitely not right. He put in a sling bag, grabbed my hand and started to sprint.

"Bryan!' I screamed "Let me go!"

"I never will," he replied back continuing to sprint and half dragging me along.

We were going way too fast and it was difficult for me to recognize where we headed towards. It got darker as we kept running and thankfully Bryan slowed down. It got darker with every step with only a few white patches of the moonlight. Giving me the hint that we were most likely in the forest. We then started to take steeper footsteps and I was sure that we were at the foot of the cliff where I had come earlier that day along with Anne, Will, Lacey and Kevin. The forest almost looked haunted, but thanks to the moon at least I could see something. This would probably be the best place in the L'Abri, having its own beauty in the morning as well as at night. Then waking up from my thoughts I looked at Bryan and stuck my tongue out.

"What the hell?" Bryan said with his face so confused that it was actually really funny.

"Thanks for embarrassing me in front of everyone Mr. coach" I said.

Bryan almost cracked up. "Oh my god Jane, still thinking about that," he said still trying to get his breath.

"First, what you did was really funny, moreover when you are embarrassed you look adorable".

I was one hundred percent sure that I was blushing and hid my face in the crook of Bryan's neck. Not that I got buttered easily, but honestly, I had no idea what this guy did to me. I stayed there for some time when Bryan asked something unusual "Jane what do you see before you release your power?".

"Oh, I see both my parents beaming at me" I replied back smiling.

"Oh" was Bryan said.

"What do you see?" I asked Bryan.

"Jane..." he began slowly. I looked right at Bryan's eyes and I could see something behind those happy and cheerful ones. Something dark, shattered and filled with sorrow.

"Um... I lost both my parents at a very young age. To be honest, I don't even remember them and right now I don't know even why I am telling you this".

He paused and I squeezed my his hand. He squeezed back and continued.

"I was left alone with my younger sister and we were raised by my uncle for a while. My sister meant the world to me and we shared a very close relationship. Then it seemed like the end of my world had come when. My sister Besse died in a car accident. She had changed at that time. Started to date this guy called Josh and both of them went to this party together and ended up pretty drunk when they were returning. Before that day Besse had always been sober, but that night she just decided to do it... Jane, she left me, left me forever and I couldn't even see her face for the last time".

He stopped and I could almost see tears near his eye and I could also see that he was trying hard to control them. I hugged him and he took his own time to let it all in.

He continued saying "L'Abri then found me and I thought I could start fresh and new. Anyway, I didn't have anything back there to live for. Things seemed to be pretty normal for around two years and then you came".

I looked up at him and he looked down at me with the faintest smile and said "Jane, I see you before I release my power".

I was pleasantly surprised at the thought that I was the one he thought about but didn't say anything, only smiled.

He suddenly jumped back. "Forget this Jane, I have something for you".

I smiled at how Bryan suddenly had a change in his mood. I saw him go towards his backpack, which he had carried along. He took out what seemed to be like two boxes. He gave one of them to me and I opened to see that they were brownies!!.

"Oh my god Bryan. I love brownies!" I exclaimed. It has been so long since I had one.

"Where did you get them from?" I asked gulping down my brownie which was heaven definitely heaven.

"Jeez Jane I know you love brownies, but honestly, women you eat like a pig." he said laughing.

I didn't mind the comment, I got it way too often.

"Oh, and I got them from the cafeteria obviously, do I look like a chef to you?".

"Nope" I said

"So why can't they give this to us everyday?" I asked.

Bryan replied saying "It's only meant for special Ultimates not for all"

"Oh please," I replied back rolling my eyes and he smiled.

I looked at the starless yet beautiful sky. While Bryan all of a sudden shifted uncomfortably and the next second I was in shock.

Chapter 16

He has come

I then saw Mal right there on top of L'Abri. Although only his face appeared it was just like how Anne had described. Bryan and I immediately got up and started to take action, but by the time we reached down the cliff Mal had already gone. I shrugged my shoulders and gave Bryan a puzzled look. We weren't sure if we should go tell the rest of the Ultimates because if he was really there, then they would have also seen him as well, or else nobody would believe us, as he was already gone. We went back up and knew it was going to be dawn soon. I lay down there on the soft grass and wondered if Anne had any visions or idea of what just happened.

Bryan then asked me "Jane do you want to sleep or run now?". Wow, what a question, I thought. I obviously was craving for some sleep right now.

"Bryan I think everyone wants and needs some rest now we'll start practicing after a while" I said, yawning.

"As you wish" Bryan replied and I managed to give him a smile. We headed back to our respective houses and as soon as I hit the bed I was deep in sleep. For a while, I didn't see anything else in my dream, but Mal's image gave me a bad feeling.

I then woke up with the sunlight burning my face moreover I was also slightly sweating. It was around 11:30, and only a few Ultimates were awake while many were still sleeping. I tried to slip back into sleep, but I could not, as it was way too hot.

So I took a shower, changed and started for the fighting arena trying not to make any sound. Before I reached the fighting arena, I heard my stomach grumble so I turned around and headed to the cafeteria hoping that there's something to eat. I reached the cafeteria to see that the Ultimates who were awake were savoring on a delicious cheese sandwich.

"Morning Jane" I heard someone say.

I looked up smiling and replied back. I grabbed a few sandwiches and finished it quickly. I scanned the crowd and saw Austin and asking him "Where's Bryan?".

"Don't know," Austin replied back, shaking his head. We waited for the rest to finish and together went to the fighting arena. Not seeing anyone we started the routine with light running around the arena with Kevin leading all of us. A few minutes later Bryan entered and was flabbergasted by what we were doing.

"Oh my god all of you are such brilliant students" he said pretending to wipe away his fake tears. Watching Bryan's drama all of us burst out laughing.

"Now serious business; today we will be learning how to use our power to it's maximum" Bryan said silencing us.

Bryan first demonstrated it to us first and then all of us took our positions having a target each in front of us. As Bryan said "Go!" I immediately thought of my parents, who always appeared beaming at me and I released my power with a thrust just like how Bryan had shown. Lots of other Ultimates also released their power, giving the arena a reddish orange glow. Most of us got it right on our first try. Although this was easier than controlling your power, but at the same more tiring. We tried once more and only the amount of glow increased. After the second attempt I was really tired and I looked at Bryan. He looked back, immediately understanding.

He then said "I know this can get tiring but let's just do this one more time perfectly give in all your energy then, I'll give you guys a break".

After Bryan finished someone in the crowd said "I can't really believe Bryan just said that, he would give us a break".

"Come on, I'm not that bad" Bryan protested.

All of us got ready, waiting for Bryan's count Fonce moreover knowing there was going to be a break afterward boosted my energy. Once again I thought of my parents and then gave in all my energy releasing my Fonce which was stronger than the previous two. I immediately fell to the ground exhausted but with satisfaction as well.

Everyone finished at the same time, so there was no waiting this time. I grabbed a bottle of water quenching my thirst and passing it on. Bryan waited for us to catch a breath, then said "I don't want you people to strain yourselves out too much but again there's a reason behind it. Yesterday some of us encountered Mal being right there, literally on top of us". Bryan paused and there was a mix of emotions. Some of us were in complete shock, while the others expressed their fear with frightened nods.

"So there's a chance he'll be there today as well and you never know he might attack anytime. Could be even now..." There were gasps everywhere. With that I request all of you to be in a condition to fight any time. Remember the safety of L'Abri lies in the hands of our house. We shall not let it down".

After that all of us exited the fighting arena and made way towards our house. I reached my bunk and Bryan was there too. I lay on my bunk without saying a word.

"Okay, I'm going out, are you coming along?" Bryan asked.

"Nope, I just want to lay down here," I said.

"Okay, but Jane please take care," Bryan said with his voice filled with concern and went out the door. What if I was the Ultimate?. This thought kept disturbing me. What if I was the destroyer for all my friends and Bryan... I let the thought sink in and got up after a few minutes for lunch. I reached the cafeteria and while I had my lunch, everyone talked about Mal although in hushed tones.

Bryan came after a while and whispered to me "Meeting after lunch, only get Anne along".

"Okay"

I finished my lunch and told Anne about the meeting after which Anne and I immediately headed towards Ellie's office. I wanted to ask Anne if she knew anything about Mal but then realized it would be brought up in the meeting anyways. After reaching Ellie's office, we saw Cara and Ellie in a conversation. We waited outside, but Cara saw us and said "Hello girls please sit down".

We took a seat and waited for Abner and Bryan to come. I looked at Ellie, who didn't seem to be in her usual happy mood. Her nose was slightly red and her head covered in her arms. Abner and Bryan came in a few minutes later. We immediately started the meeting. Ellie looked up and gave us a weak smile. She seemed like she hasn't slept for a while and something wasn't right. I wasn't really surprised after all she was the head of L'Abri, she had the responsibility to protect all of us. But I hoped apart from that there was nothing else bothering her.

Cara then spoke "Did any of you know that Mal was coming?".

All of us shook our heads, including, Anne.

"OK, that's all we wanted to know" Cara said.

"That's it then," I asked.

Cara simply nodded in response. It was surprising how the meeting was so abrupt and short. I then saw Abner, Anne and Bryan exit so I did the same. Some questions bothered me, if this was the only question why didn't they call everyone and ask? Were they suspecting Anne? Did they believe her? But I was sure when Anne said no she was obviously telling the truth besides Anne never lied. I forced the doubts out and steered towards the house, hoping to catch a full sleep. It took me a while before I could fall asleep, but on waking up it felt like I had slept only for a few minutes. I opened my eyes to see Bryan literally on top of me screaming "Get up Jane!".

I groaned and said, "Let me get a few more minutes of sleep" then Bryan said, "Jane dinner is almost over!".

"What the hell," I said immediately sitting straight and said "Let's go".

Bryan smiled and said "Wow, just that dinner did the work and over here it's been half an hour since I am trying to get you up by all other means".

I couldn't help but laugh. We reached the cafeteria with most of the Ultimates already done with eating. Thank god to some of the Ultimates who enjoyed their food for a long time, we could have our dinner. After dinner, there was a bonfire set up outside our house and everyone was there. All of us ended up playing UNO and soon found ourselves laughing at some of the stupidest jokes that Austin cracked. We played another game of UNO which was much worse than the previous game thanks to Bryan.

"Draw 2 Jane" Bryan said.

"Oh! Okay," I replied

Then Bryan said "Wait, I have another one, and another one and oh, and I almost forgot Jane I have a draw four too".

"Bryan that's not fair!" I wailed punching him in his arm. Instead of him getting him hurt, I got hurt. What was his arm made of? Metal?. As if reading my mind, Bryan gave me an innocent smile and I rolled my eyes. After the game all of us went to the places which we were assigned to guard yesterday.

Bryan and I reached our spot at the cliff. We ended staring at the sky, which was filled with stars tonight.

"Bryan do you think he'll come back today" I asked with a tinge of fear.

Bryan looked at me with courage filled in his eyes and said "Jane even if they..." then suddenly BOOM!. Bryan released a Fonce disintegrating a Presage. My eyes widened. Take the name of the devil and the devil arrives. But the thing that surprised me more was how fast Bryan was. I could hear the faint voices saying "jamais jamais, mort mort" I focused more on the sounds but they kept moving. Bryan shot another Presage,

"Bryan I can't see them" I said looking around everywhere.

"Even I can't see them Jane, you need to feel how they move. Feel the way the wind suddenly shifts and that's when you'll see them. Jane this is hard and you haven't learned it yet. I can handle them, you go and warn the rest".

No way I was going to leave Bryan alone. "I am not going anywhere" I said flatly not giving him an option but Bryan said "You are so stubborn Jane" with a slight annoyance in his voice.

That's when I saw a white, Fonce come towards me and I dodged it before it could come any closer to me. I then closed my eyes taking a deep breath. I let all the noises around me disappear. I wanted to go further and further along with the wind. Soon the noises of the Fonce, breaking down of things and Ultimates screaming started to fade. I felt the cold breeze move around me in a particular direction when suddenly I felt a shift and I quickly opened my eyes. I could partially see something hazy and shot a Fonce. The Presage disintegrated and Bryan looked at me surprised.

"Good job Jane that was really good" sounding pretty impressed.

Although the Presage didn't manage to get inside, they released a Fonce towards Ellie's office and we saw some other Ultimates manage to deflect the Fonce away. Most of the Ultimates were outside by now. Ultimates were scattered everywhere and were defending and attacking at the best.

In the mean time, I heard Abner scream "Someone let them in".

All the Ultimates gathered up and were ready to fight. It seemed like the Presage grew stronger with every blow. All of us split up, half defending and the other half attacking the Presage. I was damn exhausted but knew that I had to keep fighting no matter what. When the rays of sunlight appeared and the all the Presage were disintegrated, I let out a sigh of relief.

"All of you guys did an amazing job defending L'Abri" I heard Bryan say as we all cheered.

As the cheer came to an end, I recognized Ellie's voice and I heard her say "Like Bryan said, all you did a wonderful job. Ultimates who are injured, please go towards the infirmary where Cara and few other Soins Ultimates will be waiting. While the rest of you ought to get some rest".

After Ellie finished, I immediately looked for Anne. I found her with a bunch of other Malin Ultimates. She spotted me soon immediately rushing towards me. I looked at her and she seemed to be fine without any injuries and relief filled me.

"Jane, are you okay?" she asked with sincerity in her voice.

"Yeah, and you?" I asked

"I'm okay" Anne said reassuringly.

As I walked towards our house I thought of what Abner said. He said that someone had let them in. That Ultimate was a mole and could either save or destroy us. I climbed on my bunk and looked down to see Bryan climbing up. He climbed up and hugged me. I hugged him back feeling safe.

"Jane you were really good today. But Jane just stay safe". For the first time I saw Bryan seemed to be just as tired as I was. He didn't say another word and slept and so did I.

CHAPTER 17

DESTROYED

I woke up to the loud noises and on looking outside I saw Ultimates scattered everywhere. It was already noon and the sun was blazing. I quickly ran outside to see Mal inside. Not partially, not with his shadow, but as a whole. Standing there as a whole. I remember the first time I came back to L'Abri after the quest, it felt likeL'Abri was the only safe place after being with my parents but now I saw him here. Things were different now, we were not seeking him, rather he had invaded our safe haven.

I heard someone scream on the count of three, two, one and we all released Fonces towards Mal but he deflected it with ease.

He then scanned the crowd and said "Oh, there's my favorite" releasing a Fonce directly at Anne.

Anne saw that coming and quickly with all her power tried to stop it as beaded drops of sweat formed on her forehead. She tried harder but it was way too strong for her. Without delaying another second I then fired my Fonce and then

Mal's Fonce was gone. Anne looked at me giving me a smile and saying thank you. It looked like she wanted to say something else, but there was way too much noise, as a result I couldn't hear her.

I was about to turn and continue helping other Ultimates as well as protect L'Abri. But just when I was about to do that Anne suddenly seemed to look frightened and the next second I was on the ground. There was a slight ache in my head or else I was okay. I looked above me and Mal's white Fonce just passed so closely that I could feel the heat. Bryan was next to me with a slight cut on his head which was bleeding. "I can't lose you" was all he said and he got up continuing to fight.

Mal then asked "You liked that?"

"It only made my determination to kill you harder". I said confidently.

There was a moment of silence and then I heard Ellie say "Stop!".

All eyes were on Ellie and to my surprise Mal had stopped.

Ellie then walked towards Mal pleading "Buzz please stop all of this".

Wait, who is Buzz?. Did Ellie know Mal?. I am so confused, but looking around I realized that I wasn't the only one confused.

Mal then in a low voice said, "Ell, don't call me that" revealing his actual face, removing his green mask.

As hard as it was to admit, but he looked good. Any girl would have easily fallen for him. He had gray eyes which were as cold as ice, jet black hair, prominent cheekbones and lips which were a light shade of pink.

Mal took a step forward while Ellie fell to the ground. "Why are you doing this Buzz?. Please stop" Ellie said, pleading him with bloodshot eyes and tears running down her cheeks. "I told you to join me when things were better... Look at you now Ell. You are powerless, weak and filled with fear. I don't need you anymore" Mal said with a chill in his voice.

He then took another step forward and all of us were frozen having no idea on what was going on and what to do.

Mal then in a whisper loud enough for all of us to hear said "Ellie love never exists it's only power".

That's when he shot a Fonce at Ellie. Ellie didn't see that coming and couldn't do anything and neither could we.

The Fonce hit her and she looked directly at Mal's eyes with her last words being "Buzz I trusted you.."

Ellie started to turn pale more like as if she was terrified. Ellie turned to a stone like matter and after a few minutes disintegrated.

I asked Bryan what was happening to Ellie.

Bryan then replied "It is the worst death, worse than anyone's imagination. You could say it is your worst fear that becomes true, then it slowly eats up your soul from inside while crushing you from outside, until you die. It can happen to anyone if the Fonce hits the heart directly. The Fonce although hurts severely when in contact with the skin or any other part of the body, but when it touches the heart the pain is unbearable. For the heart is the most fragile part. The easiest to break..."

The fact that some people could be so cruel frightened me. Green scales and red eyes replaced Mal's face. He then suddenly disappeared and Presage were all around. His voice echoed "You can't get past them".

I looked around and saying that I was feeling nervous would be an understatement. Although the Presage still looked the same black and grey shadowy figures there were tons of them. Mal had lot of back up and we were only decreasing by the number not to mention that we were also getting tired by the minute. Ultimates were dying and getting injured. Our L'Abri was getting destroyed, Ellie's gone and the only hope remaining were the Ultimates remaining.

I looked up at the Presage and knew I had to continue fighting although I was craving for a break now. But if Mal won this war and got whatever he needed then he'll be merciless and will ruin the entire world. The world we were assigned to protect and make a better place. I then heard Bryan's voice in the crowd screaming "Until the very end!".

And we all shouted back "Until the very end!".

Fonces were released from both sides. All the Ultimates released Fonce after Fonce trying not to leave even a single Presage, however, the Presage were no less. I kept attacking and many Presage disintegrated. In the mean time, I would occasionally also look at Bryan who would look back and we both would nod as if it were a signal to say we were okay.

Although when I tried to look for Anne I couldn't find her in the crowd. Ultimates, Presage, weapons, broken fragments and dust covered my vision. I tired to look harder and only hoped that she was okay. For a minute I thought if she wasn't here maybe she would have made her way to the infirmary if that wasn't destroyed yet. And in that small minute span I got hit hard on my back. A sharp piercing pain exploded throughout my entire back and my legs gave in. It was as if the pain was some sort of knife which was slowly penetrating through my skin. At first I thought it was a weapon but when I got burning sensation I knew a Fonce had hit me. I fell to the ground and shut my fists and eyes as hard as I could; wanting the pain to get over. But nothing seemed to help. After a point when I couldn't take it anymore I screamed in agony. I lay still on the ground for a moment or two and then I saw my lightning bolt shine brightly and soon my pain began to subside. I rose to my feet slowly and a burst of pain erupted in back once again but I knew I had to bare with it. I couldn't be weak and I most certainly wouldn't give up.``Although the pain was still there, the anger within me vanquished it. The anger to kill those Presage who put me through so much pain and to so many other Ultimates as well. They messed with me and now it was my turn., I released my Fonce at them one after the other with much more force. After what felt like hours all the Presage were disintegrated one by one thanks to all the Ultimates. Screams and cheers of joy filled the atmosphere as we celebrated our victory although it was soon broken when Mal roared in anger, throwing his Fonces all around L'Abri.

We also started defending our land, our home by blocking the Fonces.

Cara screamed saying "Let's do this Ultimates. Ellie didn't die for nothing". This only boosted our confidence and we stuck to defending and protecting L'Abri from getting burnt down. We tried to attack Mal but he was way too strong and could easily defend our attacks. We all hoped that he was defeated since we outnumbered him and all his Presage were gone. I suddenly spotted a Fonce coming towards me and in the nick of time was able to dodge it. From the corner of my eye I then finally saw Anne who had also dodged a Fonce. A smile found its way towards my face and I knew Anne would be fine. I continued to defend till my last breath.

Although the Fonce had taken away a lot of my energy my lightning bolt had made subsided the pain by now. I blocked Mal's Fonce coming towards some other Ultimates. Just then one of Mal's Fonce came towards me and I dodged it with Alex helping me. I thanked him and he just smiled.

Just then my eyes spot a Mal's Fonce which was directly headed towards Anne. It was way too close to Anne and by the time I could release my Fonce Mal's Fonce would have hit her. Then I saw Will jump in front of Anne, as a result the Fonce hit Will in his chest and he was immediately on the ground. Anne froze and all of us were in shock.

"Not in a million years have we seen any sacrifice like this" I heard Abner say.

Anne knelt down beside Will's body holding his hand with tears flowing down her face. Will grasping for his last breath said "Anne, I had always loved…" Anne kissed him on the forehead and Will died away with a smile on his face. I couldn't help but let a tear slip away from my eyes.

«*Will est mort mais avec une bonne mort avec fierté* » I heard Bryan say while the crowd cheered. « *le ciel lui prend* » Cara said and instead of Will becoming stone like he turned into gold ash and flew away into the sky. I didn't understand what they said or why Will died this way, but I knew he was happy where ever he was now.

Mal without wasting any time threw another Fonce towards Anne but Bryan turned out to be quicker than Mal thus

---

* *Will est mort mais avec une bonne mort avec fierté* ~ *Will died a good death and with pride.*
  le ciel lui prend ~ *the heaven take him.*

intercepting the Fonce. I looked at Bryan with great fullness and he smiled back at me. Anne had tears rushing through her eyes and started walking forward towards Mal.

"Stop Anne!" I said, hoping that she wouldn't do what I thought she was about to do. Anne looked at me and shook her head. Anne took a step closer and Mal released a Fonce towards her which she parried. He released another Fonces, but this time he put out two. One of which I immediately deflected while she dodged the other one. Now I could see Mal getting annoyed and threw a numerous amount of Fonces directly at Anne which all of us helped Anne to dodge.

"Aaahh" Mal screamed "I want her dead and she will die. Without her all of you are nothing". He then released a black Fonce towards Anne which was much faster than the normal Fonce. All of us then deflected it, but it only grew bigger and split up zooming in every direction. One mistake of deflecting them and they only grew stronger.

We had no other option but to run for as long as we could. Everyone seemed to be helpless. Bryan grabbed my arm and we ran towards the black Fonces instead running past them. This was much easier and I saw Kevin along with the other Ultimates follow the same thing. I wanted to tell Anne to do the same thing, but instead of running she released a Fonce towards Mal. Mal was caught by surprise and it hit him.

He froze for a minute and Anne said "Mal you might have frightened us with that black Fonce of yours but it has drained the power from you. I won't let you hurt any of the Ultimates. I won't let you destroy more of L'Abri. And moreover, I won't let you touch Jane".

I was touched by what Anne had said but then I saw a black Fonce come towards Anne. I ran and Bryan saw that too. We sprinted towards Anne and pushed Anne. The black ball flew past us. As we got up another black ball hit Anne from behind. Neither did I see that coming nor did Anne. As soon as it hit Anne she shrieked with pain.

"Annnnnnne!" I screamed.

"No this couldn't be happening" I thought. "It is a dream, this wasn't possible. I know Anne wouldn't leave me like that", these thoughts ran through my mind.

Instead of Anne falling to the ground, she floated in mid air. She turned bright white and released Fonces which disintegrated all the black balls. Anne released white, Fonce towards Mal which wrapped around him.

Anne's voice echoed around him as she said "Mal you're a coward, a traitor. You controlled people through their weakness, their fear. I am no longer scared of you as You used your loved ones. You were never brave and you never conquered over anyone because they are all dead".

"Nooo!" Mal shrieked. It sounded like he was gasping for air. "Release me, I'll leave and won't ever come back" Mal said with more difficulty as every second passed.

"Your own fear has killed you Mal" Anne said and with a blast of white light Mal was gone. Only shreds of his mask and some ashes left while the rest disintegrated.

Anne fell to the ground while tele light was all around the attic. I ran towards Anne, who was fighting to breathe.

"Jane, I am so sorry... be stronger than me.." and her eyes closed, closed forever...

I was crying "Anne please don't go" I whispered softly.

Arms wrapped around me from behind and I sank into them.

I let the tears flow and Bryan softly said "Be strong Jane".

I stopped and looked around. The houses were all wrecked, the cafeteria and Ellie's office was destroyed. L'Abri was ravaged and in flames. Abner then took the lead and the rest of the Ultimates, who were alive followed. It didn't take me long to recognize that we headed towards the university. The elevators weren't working, no surprise on that, so we took the stairs and headed straight to the attic hoping Sacre was there.

As we climbed higher we passed labs. Fluids were scattered everywhere along with broken test tubes and various other chemical equipments which I didn't recognize. On reaching the next floor I recognized a very familiar room. It was the room where we would have done the analytical thinking test. All the fun Anne and I had the other day chasing each other. The thought of Anne quickly sent pained feeling through me. The fact that she wasn't there immediately brought tears to my eyes, which I brushed away before anyone else could see.

I looked up to see that we had reached the attic. Without Ellie and with L'Abri destroyed, there was no place to go and the least we could ask for was Sacre. As we entered Abner motioned for us to sit with only Bryan, Cara and Abner standing. I looked around to see Lacey seated next to Kevin in tears while Kevin comforted her. I then saw Austin sitting in the corner and sat next to him.

He saw me and gave me a small smile. Austin looked pale with his cheeks trailed with remains of tears. The humor was wiped from him and I thought even during this serious time he would be cracking jokes. He looked at me with tears brimming in his eyes and he softly said "I am sorry for Anne...".

I nodded in response trying to hide away my own tears. I then began to say "Austin I.." but my voice trailed off as he began to speak. His voice was so soft and hurt, it hurt me more to hear him like that.

"Alex was my best buddy, my only true friend here, someone who I could confide in. The only one who wouldn't mind, however crazy, I got and we had true Bromance". I would never imagine Austin say anything that deep and I knew it came right from his heart. I had no words and we just remained silent. Alex was also gone and the last time I saw him was when he helped me. Sometimes only silence was golden and it's the only thing you'll need. Silently accepting the truth and moving on.

"Be stronger than me Jane..." her last words echoing in my ears and I wanted her to know that's exactly what I 'll do.

Cara's voice, then brought me back to reality, the reality which wasn't worth living in anymore. "It'll only be fair for all of us to ask Sacre together".

On the count of three two one and together we all chorused "Sacre can you please help us?". The familiar tele mist filled the room once again while Bryan sat next to me. I sank into his shoulder with slow tears still flowing. As I thought may be the truth that Anne isn't here anymore, will take some time for me to reconcile with, may be an eternity.

"I don't have much time my brave Ultimates. I had gone, then because of the prophecy. The destined Ultimate was Ellie..."

There was a gasp and hushed whispers filled the room. I wondered who I should talk to since Anne wasn't there and Bryan spoke to Abner.

"Anne was the bravest of all. She wasn't the chosen Ultimate but decided to become the Savior. She died without any fear. Fearless almost you could say. She protected her loved ones and that's how she was able to overpower Mal. As you all must know by now Mal had a peculiar way of fighting. He would penetrate through one's brain find your worst fears and scare you, thus rendering you powerless. Ellie's worst fear was to see L'Abri and all of you hurt. And when she saw all of you hurt, other Ultimates and L'Abri getting destroyed right in front of her eyes she broke down and couldn't take it anymore. She had become way beyond weak.

On the contrary, Anne was afraid of losing her loved ones and not being able to protect them. After Jane almost got hurt while trying to protectAnne, gave her a silent rage. Not to mention Will's death made her even angrier. She turned her fear into her strength so that she wouldn't have to see any more deaths. She was the only one who correctly guessed what Mal feared the most, her fearlessness. Anne was so special because she realized what was right and what was wrong.

She was intelligent in her own way which scared Mal. Mal not only feared Anne's fearlessness but also the fact that he could lose. Anne used both of them against him and thus overpowering him. Nobody can be fearless but it matters how you handle you fear. There was a minute of silence as we paid tribute to the ones who had lost their lives protecting us and L'Abri.

The memories with Anne came in my mind like a fast movie.

Sacre then said "I would like to apologize to all of you for all the pain you have gone through and the loss of your fellow

mates and loved ones. I believe that you all have the right
know something. Most of you must be knowing that I was
the first Ultimate. And you must also be knowing that my
last wish was to stay and look after all of you. It happened
years ago when Ellie and Mal were students just like you at
L'Abri.

They trained together and were inseparable. His name was
Buzz back then. Both of them were able fighters and shared a
strong bond. But then days passed and Buzz wondered what
more?. His greed for power led to his death. He decided to
leave L'Abri and at that time I hadn't given him anything
which would erase his memories of L'Abri. Which was why
he remembered all about L'Abri and his powers and used it
to his advantage.

I was then cursed by them. You could imagine them as the
gods, goddesses, angels, fairies and what not. I was cursed
because one of our own had turned upon us and I was
the one to be blamed. I was trapped in this box after that
incident. And all I hope is that you could all forgive me..."

The mist, then disappeared with Sacre not giving us any
actual suggestion. A part of me did feel sympathetic towards
Sacre. All those years in that box and all the guilt he must
still be living with.

We walked out despite not knowing where to go. I went
along with Bryan where ever he planned to go. Images of
Anne flooded my mind, right from being small kids to the
last words she told me, be stronger than I was.." everything

kept on coming back in cycles and tears flowed freely from my eyes. We were in the cliff and I couldn't have asked for a better place. Without Anne how would I survive my summers?, what would I tell aunty and uncle once I got back?. I felt incomplete like as if the most important part of my being was cut away from me. I let the thoughts just sink in and looked up to see the clear sky. That's when I felt warm and I saw Bryan hug me from behind. Maybe I wasn't alone after all. Bryan was always there for me. He then turned to look at me directly in the eyes, softly brushing my lips and whispering "Jane We'll find a way out of this. Together I promise..."